"Ever-intelligent horror nov... story—true as far as the part... geist.... More artful, if less e... bloodsucker operas—but all...

—... (pointer review)

"Remarkable and well told... The final pages are especially moving, and offer a potent thesis for what we have come to refer to as poltergeist phenomena."
—Douglas E. Winter, *The Magazine of Fantasy & Science Fiction*

"Monahan keeps a perfect feeling of the period and his spooky story unfolds with just the proper sort of pacing.... The author has set himself a neat little challenge, met it completely, and produced an altogether entertaining book."
—Gahan Wilson, *Realms of Fantasy*

"Monahan, author of, among a variety of other novels, the modern vampire classic *The Book of Common Dread*, has taken what is presumably a piece of real history and transformed it, with the storyteller's skill, into a highly speculative fictional interpretation. Now whether the historical base for Monahan's novel is real or not, beats me. But the idea of a nineteenth-century *Amityville Horror* is a great conceit in any case."
—Edward Bryant, *Locus*

"The manuscript is an excellent historical document, rich in period detail.... It's a whodunit, whatdunit, and whydunit all rolled into one."
—*Horror*

"An atmospheric and observant narrative... Too compelling to put down, all the more so because of its real-life 'X-File' quality (you can even visit the spot where it all took place, in Robertson County, TN). Whether you believe or doubt the story, it will certainly enthrall you... and most likely keep you up at night, too."
—Ali Lerner, *Fangoria*

Also by Brent Monahan

DeathBite (with Michael Maryk) (1979)
Satan's Serenade (1989)
The Uprising (1992)
The Book of Common Dread (1993)
The Blood of the Covenant (1995)
The Jekyl Island Club (2000)

AN AMERICAN HAUNTING

The Bell Witch

Being the
Eye Witness Account of
Richard Powell
Concerning the Bell Witch Haunting
of Robertson County, Tennessee
1817–1821

edited by
Brent Monahan

St. Martin's Griffin ♙ New York

Design by Nancy Resnick

Edited by Gordon Van Gelder

www.stmartins.com

Library of Congress Cataloging-in-Publication Data

Monahan, Brent.
   An American haunting: the Bell witch / by Brent Monahan.
      p.   cm.
   ISBN-10 0-312-15061-X (hc)
   ISBN-10 0-312-36353-2 (pbk)
   ISBN-13 978-0-312-36353-6
      1. Poltergeists—Tennessee—Robertson County—Fiction.
   2. Bell family—Fiction. 3. Ghosts—Tennessee—Robertson
   County—Fiction.   I. Title.
   PS3565.05158B45   1997
   813'.54—dc20   96-43935
                                                            CIP

First published by St. Martin's Press under the title *The Bell Witch*

First St. Martin's Griffin Edition: May 2006

10 9 8 7 6 5 4 3 2 1

Hell hath no limits, nor is circumscribed
In one self-place; for where we are is Hell,
And where Hell is, there must we ever be.

— Christopher Marlowe, *Faustus*

Editor's Preface

The story of the Bell Witch is true. My task is to convince you to believe this, in spite of the fact that you may know me to be a writer of supernatural fiction. Unless I succeed, you will be cheated of the experience of wonder and terror that the tale should rightly produce.

This event from the early days of wilderness America involved real people and real places. You can do as I did and visit Adams, Tennessee, where you can stand before the graves of many of those involved in the Bell Witch haunting. You can visit the archives of Tennessee and satisfy yourself that the author of the narrative that follows was an actual state politician in the first half of the nineteenth century.

Although this story is not of my invention, it is because I am a "horror" writer that I became involved early in bringing to light the manuscript that follows. While I was pursuing my doctorate in music from Indiana University, Bloomington, I developed a close friendship with another student, Clarissa Davenport Behr. She has since also received her doctorate in music and has married. Clarissa Davis resides in Vicksburg,

Mississippi, where she grew up. We have stayed in touch over the years.

In January 1995, another friend of Mrs. Davis, who lives in Port Gibson, Mississippi, discovered an old manuscript in the attic of a recently deceased aunt. At the time of its discovery the manuscript was sealed inside a large envelope, and it, in turn, had been protected by a sizable, unsealed folder. The sealed manuscript was accompanied by a time-yellowed, tri-folded sheet of linen paper. Upon breaking the outer envelope's seal and reading the full contents of the folder, Mrs. Davis's friend "got scared so bad I couldn't sleep for three nights." The author of this long-forgotten manuscript seemed sincere, yet the man's tale was of such stark horror that the woman hoped it was just an unpublished flight of fantasy. Having little formal education, she was at a loss over how to begin verifying its authenticity. She confided her find to Mrs. Davis, who asked and was given permission to read the materials. Not far into her reading, Mrs. Davis thought of me as a person well qualified to get to the bottom of the mystery. My skills at academic research and immersion as a fiction author into the subjects of ghosts, hauntings, and the like recommended me to deal with the subject matter. I was mailed a photocopy of the pages, likewise read the contents with skepticism, and set out to see if there was any way they could be true.

I paid a telephone visit to the woman who had discovered the materials. Like Mrs. Davis, she is a Daughter of the American Revolution and a Colonial Dame and can trace her heritage back many generations. From her I was able to get enough facts to determine that the writer of the manuscript, her distant relative, was a Richard Powell, who was born in Virginia in 1788 and who died somewhere near Springfield, Tennessee, in 1842.

Starting with this scant knowledge I began my investigation and lucked upon a "vanity press" history of that area by a local historian.[1] It seems that in 1816, Powell had come to an area of Middle Tennessee called Red River (renamed Adams Station in 1859 with the coming of the Louisville & Nashville Railroad and later simply Adams). Powell was briefly an educator during that community's adolescence. Although no longer teaching in the area, in 1824 he married a former pupil, Elizabeth Bell. Known as Betsy, she was the second daughter of John Bell, a prominent Red River farmer. On page 159 of the Winters history, the author writes, "The name of Jon [sic] Bell has been associated with the legend of the 'Bell Witch' down through the past 150 years." Already, a corner of the puzzle had fallen into place.

I began calling antiquarian and Tennesseeana book shops in Nashville and in Montgomery and Robertson Counties. The proprietors were very helpful, and in quick order I owned no fewer than six books detailing information on this Bell Witch legend. Most of these books contain an identical set of woodcut drawings based on the haunting, and some of these are presented throughout this volume as well. These six local publications all describe a haunting in Adams that took place more than 170 years ago and which became "world famous." While the older members of the Bell family and their friends had sought diligently to keep a lid on the happenings, eventually one of the youngest sons assembled a notebook on the event,[2] and a child of another son wrote his recollections of

[1]Ralph L. Winter, *Historical Sketches of Adams/Robertson County, Tennessee and Port Royal/Montgomery County, Tennessee/From 1779 to 1968* (2nd printing; Clarksville, Tenn.: Samuel J. Winters, 1978).
[2]Richard Williams Bell, *The Bell Witch or Our Family Trouble, 1846* (Mini-Histories: Nashville, 1985).

his father, John Bell, Jr., from approximately the year 1884.[3] A work published in the 1890s not only reprints *Our Family Trouble,* the Richard Williams Bell account, but also supplies a wealth of background history and personal recollections of many people of the community who witnessed the haunting.[4] I am not overstating the case in saying that more than once the hair stood up on the nape of my neck as one book after the next echoed the events in Powell's manuscript, detail for detail.

The Bell Witch incident falls under the classification of a poltergeist haunting. According to yet another book I found that included the Bell Witch story with other similar occurrences, a poltergeist (meaning literally "racket-making ghost" in German) is a "frisky, mischievous, unseen spirit that specializes in knocking on walls, tossing things like crockery about, and performing other supernatural feats. In the scientific sense, there is no such thing as a poltergeist. There is only poltergeist activity . . . odd things that happen due to some unknown force or power, perhaps psychological in nature."[5]

Poltergeist hauntings have been recorded in Western civilization from as far back as A.D. 355. In North America, well-documented incidents have occurred in Stratford, Connecticut, in 1850; Macon, Georgia, in 1870; Amherst, Nova Scotia, in 1878; and Seaford, Long Island, in 1958. Two important elements make the Bell haunting different from all oth-

[3]Charles Bailey Bell, M.D., *The Bell Witch of Tennessee* (n.p., 1934; facsimile reproduction by Charles Elder, Bookseller: Nashville, 1972).
[4]M. V. Ingram, *Authenticated History of the Bell Witch/And Other Stories of the World's Greatest Unexplained Phenomenon* (M. V. Ingram: Clarksville, Tenn., 1894; facsimile reproduction by Rare Book Reprints: Nashville, 1961).
[5]David C. Knight, *Poltergeists: Hauntings and the Haunted* (Philadelphia: J. B. Lippincott Co., 1972).

ers. The first is that this is the only known incident in which the spirit took credit for killing someone. Astounding as this detail is, a much more gruesome element is revealed by the manuscript of Richard Powell . . . and by his words alone.

All of the books I found came into existence after the creation of Powell's biographical account of the incident, and he clearly did not anticipate them. Since he wrote, dated, and sealed his manuscript before any of the other texts were written, none could have influenced his retelling. This argues strongly for its authenticity.

Elizabeth Bell Powell died in 1890, at the age of eighty-five, having survived her husband by almost five decades. After Richard's death, she and her daughter, whose first name I have yet to learn but who was curiously alleged to have married a Zadok Bell, moved to Panola County, Mississippi. This is evidently how the manuscript and letter got to that state from Tennessee. As the other members of her family had, Betsy jealously guarded the secrets of the Bell Witch haunting and never spoke of it. She did, however, threaten to sue the *Saturday Evening Post* in 1849 for publishing falsehoods concerning the affair. The magazine printed an apology and retraction. I reported all these findings to Mrs. Davis and her friend.

Just about every published author of fiction, reportage, or biography has at one time or another been approached by someone having "the most unique idea for a novel" or a life that "my friends tell me just must be made into a book." These people generally offer to split future profits in exchange for writing talents they lack. I have been thus approached several times and on each occasion declined the honor. When I was asked to shepherd this manuscript into publication, however, I had no misgivings. The manuscript and my own research had turned me into a believer. The main stipulation of the agreement was that I not reveal the name of the woman who owns

5

the original manuscript. She understands well the reason the old Bell family worked so diligently to put a tight lid on the incident; much annoyance and loss of privacy can come from the publication of this bizarre, horrifying story.

Despite the claim of M. V. Ingram and others that this event is "world famous," the fact that all the detailed books I read about it were printed and reprinted within forty miles of Adams speaks otherwise. I believe that this story is, in fact, known by few and deserves greater fame. Among the several remembrances of the Bell Witch incident, the most shocking revelations are recounted only in Richard Powell's version. Once you read his words, you will realize that a modern repetition of this phenomenon is not beyond possibility, and that greater awareness of this event could actually save physical and mental lives.

As a final step in the process of investigating this real-life mystery, I visited Adams, Tennessee. There is little left beyond gravestones to see. The town is almost too small to deserve a name. Farming is clearly still the source of livelihood, as it was in John and Betsy Bell's time. A part of the original Bell farmland is owned and worked by Walter and Chris Kirby. Chris was kind enough to spend the better part of a cold hour on her front porch talking to this unexpected visitor about the legend. The Kirbys augment their income in the nonrainy season by showing the "Bell Witch cave," which is mentioned in Richard Powell's testimony and in Charles Bailey Bell's account as well. While professing not to be superstitious, Mrs. Kirby will not go into the cave alone. She tells of one incident in which a translucent mass "like a giant bubble" approached and went through her while she was conducting a tour and that it rendered her sick for some hours. She also tells of noises heard periodically in the cave but readily admits that such strange happenings may be caused by gases and water percolating through the pervious limestone rock. Of the Bell farm where the haunting mostly took place, all that remains are stone foundations, bases of chimneys, and a decrepit man-made hole that was probably a well. No one has ever contemplated rebuilding there since its abandonment.

Since neither physical clues nor living witnesses remain, we must rely on the written accounts of those who were there. You are about to read how Richard Powell, as a learned man educated in the Age of Enlightenment, as a close friend of the Bell family but not a member, and as a man smitten by the bedeviled Betsy Bell, was uniquely positioned to be *the* definitive chronicler of this horrific incident. Most astonishing, you will eventually learn why the man was compelled to write a story he had wholeheartedly hoped he could shove into a dark recess of his memory and forget.

In order to keep the sealed manuscript isolated as a tale, I want to end this introduction by giving you the contents of the letter that accompanied it. One other fact is vital for you to know first: in 1837, when Richard was forty-nine and had been married to Betsy for thirteen years, he suffered a massive stroke and nearly died. It was not solely the prospect of impending death, however, that compelled Powell to write this narrative, as you will learn.

The letter inside the folder was written on linen paper bearing a watermark common in the first half of the nineteenth century. When unfolded, it revealed "post-Colonial cursive" penmanship and had clearly been written with a quill-type pen. Mr. Powell served for a time as a state senator in Tennessee. Political documents written by him are available at the University of Tennessee, Knoxville, archive. They conform to the handwriting of both the letter and manuscript.

Two lines were inscribed on the outer side of the letter, about twice as large as the rest. They read:

7

The inside words read:

November, 1841

With this letter you will find a packet of paper, sealed up. Do not open it so long as your mother remains untroubled. Should unexplained noises or other unnatural occurrences begin around her or if she begins to have fits or fainting spells, then you and you alone must open this envelope and study its contents. At that point, you will need to enlist the help of others. Whether you choose to share the contents with your mother before securing that help I leave to your judgement. Know that I love you and your mother as I do life itself, and that wherever my immortal spirit resides I shall be praying for your happiness.

Father

Brent Monahan
Yardley, Pa.

You first heard about the "Bell witch" when you were seven. At that time and ever since, your mother and I have insisted to you that it was a tall tale invented by our neighbours where we used to live. This is not so. Now you must learn the truth of it, in every detail. Let me begin with a most important event in the shaping of this sad and shocking story.

The invisible creature that haunted your mother and the rest of the Bell family was originally called by people in Red River "Kate Batts's witch," or simply "Old Kate." Mrs. Batts herself was the cause of this ignorance.

In the year 1818 Kate Batts was, I judge, about forty years old. She possessed no greater height than most women but certainly greater girth. The flesh of her upper arms was as thick as a young man's thighs. She also possessed enormous quantities of bright red hair and freckles, but it was not her size, her crowning glory, nor her mottled skin that frightened most persons in her presence; it was rather her behaviour. Mrs. Batts displayed the most forceful and extravagant of personalities I ever encountered. She felt nothing by halves. Nor would she conceal her passions but seemed ever eager to strop her sharp tongue against the sensibilities of women and men alike.

Some said that she had not always been so outspoken. Her character, they claimed, had hardened when her husband, Frederik, became a total invalid. The trunk of a tree he was felling kicked back and crushed his legs. This forced an already hard-working woman to shoulder also the manly duties of their farm. She acquitted herself well, but many supposed this was at the sacrifice of a clement nature. Others swore that she had always had "things flying around loose in her belfry" and that it had been ordained in heaven that she should wed herself to the name Batts. I try to temper my judgement of others, but I freely admit she never seemed less than odd to me. For example, she unflaggingly pushed her ungainly sons, Jack and Calvin (everyone called the pair Jack and the Beanstalk), upon the eligible young women of Red River. "Keep your eyes set on Calvin, girls," she would crow. "He's all warp and no fillin', but once you own him, you can weave him a yard wide." Of Jack she would say, "You never mind that his right eye wanders a bit. It's wandering to spy business opportunities, not loose women."

A small group thought Kate Batts a witch even before the portentous event I am about to relate. Their first reason was that she owned a perfectly good mare but never rode it. Superstitious folks swear that horses will not abide witches on their backs, compelling them to travel by broomstick. The second reason arose from her constant circuit of the farms within the region, buying up from the other wives surplus wool, cotton and flax, to keep her Negro women busy from dawn to dusk spinning, weaving and knitting. In exchange for the many opinions and tidbits of gossip she lavished upon the other wives, she begged free pins and needles. Most of us assumed that this was yet one more of her tricks for pinching pennies and keeping the wolf from the Battses' door. Many old wives, however, declared that witches begged pins to get power, that a pin freely given could be stuck later into a carved or sewn likeness to torment its donor's flesh.

All these contributed to both the naming of the spirit, and to Kate Batts's undoing in the community, yet no action condemned her so much as her behaviour on a Wednesday in May, 1818. Sister Batts proudly displayed a God-fearing Christian attitude and was a charter member of the Red River Baptist Church. It was freely granted that she had never been cited for absence of a Sunday and was the loudest singer and the most vocal in the Amens, even though she not once arrived before the middle of the service. A good deal of what I have already written (as much of this testament must perforce be) is only hearsay, but at this event I was personally in attendance.

The matter occurred at a revival at Fort's meeting house. The leader was a celebrated revivalist of that time by the name of Rev. Thomas Felts. In those days not one in ten settlers in Middle Tennessee took membership in a church or society, most having come west to find land, not religion. By that reckoning, Red River was among the most godly of communities, and yet we possessed our generous share of the wicked and unwashed. At least a dozen of this number were at the revival, including a few darkies who occupied the southeast corner of the house, which was their allowed space.[1]

II

Rev. Felts had arrived the previous Sunday. The meeting commenced on Monday and was scheduled to last until Friday evening. By late Wednesday, Brother Felts's relentless depictions of eternal damnation had whipped our souls into various degrees of agitation, and among these was a virtuoso sinner by the name of Joe Edwards, who jumped up to proclaim his repentance. I kept my place on a bench in the northeast corner while well-intentioned neighbours swept towards the pulpit to help Brother Felts claim Mr. Edwards's soul for Jesus. There were choruses of hallelujahs and much laying-on of hands. Of a sudden, Joe fell to all fours, grabbed the anxious seat,₂ and began howling.

It was at that moment that Kate Batts made her predictably late entrance to the meeting, led by her Negro maid Phyllis and flanked by two of her black boys. For whatever spiritual reason, clear only to Sister Batts, she chose to break through the circle of faithful, rush upon the prostrate man, throw her great riding skirt over his back and head, and plop her mass fully upon him, belling with a noise that made Mr. Edwards's howls sound like whimpers.

Everyone's prayers stopped instantly, such was the shock of the congregation. Kate, however, continued to bellow, and the benighted sinner beneath her was convinced that the Devil himself had claimed him.

"Lord, save me! Sweet Jesus, lift Satan off me, or I will surely sink down to eternal torment!" cried Mr. Edwards, or words to that effect. He was difficult to understand, what with Kate Batts's barking.

By the time the poor man had exhausted his breath, I had moved myself directly behind Mrs. Batts, tapped her on the shoulder, and suggested that she might better assist the man's salvation from a bench. She refused.

"No, thank you, Perfessor Powell," she told me. "This altitude is so consoling to my disposition that I feel amply corrugated." To add to her imperfections, the woman sought grandeur through speaking large words she either invented or misused, oblivious to the fact that it fooled no one in the community.

"But, Sister Batts, the mourner is suffocating," Rev. Felts protested.

"Yes indeed, let him suffocate, Preacher," she answered. "I am helping him get closer to the Lord."

By this time, even the most pious of the congregants could not help but see humour in the situation. I was one who helped lift Mrs. Batts off the sinner just as his strength gave way. Those who had not already left the building to politely dispel their laughter were quickly dismissed by Rev. Felts, who was wise enough to adjourn the saving of souls until the morrow. One man stood in the meeting house with a wrathful face, towering over the seated Mrs. Batts.

"Is it not enough that you belittle worship of the Almighty by your constant lateness, woman? Must you also make a mockery of a man's awakening to the light?"

I was one of several who turned at the rebuke. On normal occasions your grandfather Bell was a commanding figure of a man. He stood a bit over six feet but seemed even taller, as his frame was lank. Also, despite his sixty-eight years, his build was sinewy. He had a long and angular face, with ears that stuck far out, a large nose, and a thin-lipped mouth, making his countenance never the most restful of sights. At this moment, however,

13

he looked like Moses come down from Mount Sinai to find the Israelites worshipping the golden calf.

"You dare to exscalpitate me, John Bell?" Mrs. Batts said, returning your grandfather's glare with a defiant look of her own. "Take the log from your own eye, sinner, that ye shall see clearly to remove the mole from mine! If this meetin' had been convenienced at Red River Church you wouldn't even be welcome to attend."

I heard a small gasp at my left and looked for its source. There stood your mother, her blue eyes wide open in shock, her porcelain complection [sic] turned even more pale. In keeping with the nature of the revival, she wore a simple linsey-woolsey dress without ribbons or lace, and yet she was exquisite to look upon. At her sides stood her similarly aghast companions, Theny Thorn and Becky Porter. They were both her senior, yet Betsy looked more mature than either. She was just shy of thirteen years.

The cause of the collective gasp was Kate Batts's public reminder of John Bell's expulsion from the Red River Baptist Church. This had happened in January of 1818, soon after he had been convicted of usury by a jury in Robertson County Circuit Court.

The Bells and the Battses owned adjacent lands. A few days after Frederik Batts was laid low by the tree, John offered a sum of money for an unused parcel of the Batts farm. His motivation, he affirmed to his other neighbours, was selfless. It made perfect sense to me. Since Frederik was now helpless to farm, the Batts family would have far greater need of cash than of spare land. Stipulations of the agreement were that John also would sell the Battses a Negro male to help perform Frederik's physical duties and also to make a loan of cash. Grandfather Bell was known to be a shrewd businessman, but in this instance he made the mistake of not specifying in a written contract the rate of interest for the darkie and the cash. Kate publicly challenged the rate she was paying. Despite the court's findings, most of the community felt that John had been punished beyond the serving of justice. Nevertheless, once the law of the county had passed judgement, John's fellow elders of Red River Baptist felt they had no choice but to expel him. He was welcome at every other church in the region, and all pastors, including his old reverend, Sugg Fort, called constantly at his home. The shame, however, remained a thorn that could not be removed from his side.

"Misquote the Bible as much as you like, woman," John said. "It will make you no less the lying witch that you are."

Sister Batts gathered up her riding skirt with a swipe of her hand, marched to the meeting house's main door, pivoted about, and delivered the words that were surely her undoing and, I fear, the herald of disaster to the Bell family.

"Witch, am I? Then let me offer you a witch's malefaction, Old John Bell: You may have your broad acres as well as mine, purchased at a penitence. You may have your big house and your salubricated health right now. But just wait and see what sad changes shall soon descend upon you. And more than you among the Bells."

She uttered a bray of triumph and stomped out into the coming dusk. I turned my attention back on your mother, who was by now ashen-faced. I bade her sit before she fell into a swoon.

"Pay her no mind, Betsy," I counseled. "She is only an addlebrained woman, to be pitied."

"Pitied," John said to me, "but not humoured."

15

I was glad to note that only a hand full [sic] had remained inside the meeting house to witness the incident. I walked to the door, to catch some fresh air. Phyllis had already unhitched the old, perpetually unridden horse and was leading it homeward at a good clip, with Mrs. Batts and the rest of what we called "Kate's troop" marching behind. I recount this incident at the start of my writing for sober purpose. Remember well the woman's curse and the effect it produced upon your mother!

"Has she not cursed me enough with her suit?" fumed your grandfather to me as he quit the meeting house. "The Lord has surely turned his back upon me. How have I profited from that land? What has it been used for but your sustenance and the good of our children?"

I and the children were indeed the only benefactors of the parcel of land at that time. It had been provided for my use, along with the two-room log cabin that served double purpose as my living quarters and school house. I was then only the second teacher in that area of Tennessee and Kentucky.[3] You know my history well enough, so that I only need remind you that I was born in March of 1788, the same month and year that the ill-fated state of Franklin came to an end.[4] Note the date of my birth, as it also bears significance in this terrible tale.

I arrived in Nashville from across the Alleghenies in July of 1815. I found it a wilderness of Philistines and transients, not the most receptive location in which to fulfill my life's calling. I had been informed there, however, that among the many growing backwoods communities surrounding Nashville, Red River was the most religious and the most eager for book learning. This was proven swiftly upon my arrival, as I was briefly interviewed by several worthies of the community (your

grandfather Bell being among them) and hired with en-
thusiasm. They rightly believed that if our new republic
was to flourish based upon the consent of the common
man, all citizens were obliged to be educated participants.
John Bell, Sr. became my champion, lending out land
close by the Red River upon which a schoolhouse might
be erected and signing a subscription for his daughter,
Elizabeth, whom everyone called Betsy. In quick fashion,
I had all the pupils I could accommodate, including Partheny Thorn, Rebecca Porter, Piety Horn Fort, Felix
Northington, George Wimberly, Alexander Gooch, Law-
son Fort, and, on occasion, a handsome young man
named Joshua Gardner.

Had Sister Batts remained inside Fort's meeting house
to hear John Bell's complaints to me that evening, I know
she would have had a ready retort. While lending out the
land for a schoolhouse, John still owned it nonetheless.
Moreover, he had managed to have the community pitch
in and erect a large building which could be used for
other purpose in case the teaching venture failed. Also, I
used what little spare time I possessed to clear part of the
land for crops, saving John's family and slaves the labour
of felling trees and burning stumps. These attributed mo-
tivations would be unkind were it not for my conviction
that this was the very way John Bell's mind worked,
crediting such thinking to good business sense. No one,
however, could gainsay that he had donated the land and
contributed logs and the sweat of his own brow.

Before I continue, I must describe Red River. Even
though it lies but twelve miles north of Springfield, we
were careful never to bring you through that area, for
fear of your hearing parts of this very tale. Friends and
relatives still living there have always visited us. Those

17

who love or those since departed who loved your mother entered into a common pact of silence concerning that period, since all realized that only sorrow or worse could result from its disinterment. Nevertheless, there are many all around Red River eager to bend any passer-by's ear with not only remembrances but the wildest embellishments and outright lies about the incident, and I would not chance exposing either you or your mother to this. I need to describe the place also because I have traveled through there recently, and even in this short time much has vanished.

Your grandfather John Bell was born in Halifax County, North Carolina, in 1750. He was of Scottish stock. When he was young he apprenticed to become a cooper, but he found a greater aptitude in the land and determined to be a farmer. He got himself a small farm but then had the great fortune to woo and wed Miss Lucy Williams of Edgecombe County, North Carolina, descendant of venerable English stock and daughter of a John Williams, who, I am told, had amassed in his lifetime considerable wealth. This wedding took place in 1782. Your grandfather was thirty-two and your grandmother was twelve years old at the time.

At the turn of the century, word came back monthly from the newly opened Indian territories concerning the ability to acquire huge tracts of land for tiny amounts of money. In 1804 John moved his family to Red River, where several families from Edgecombe County had already settled. He purchased about 1,000 acres, just above Brown's Ford and on a high bluff overlooking a bend in the Red River itself. The area had another name: the Barren Plains. Why it was called thus is confusion to me, as this was among the most fertile and level land in all of

Middle Tennessee. The river ran strong, providing water and rich bottom land in the driest months. Timber was more than plentiful. Fish and game abounded. There were even numerous caves for ready-made cold storage. One might have lived contented on the great variety of native nuts, grapes, and berries alone. It was as close to a new Eden as any man or woman could expect, and yet if the advances of civilization were suddenly required the village of Port Royal lay only seven miles west and the town of Nashville forty miles south.

At the time your grandfather and his family arrived, a one-and-a-half-story house already existed on the land. It was a double-length hewn log structure, with wide hall-ways above and below in between and wide doors front and back to coax the breeze through in summer. There was a chimney at either end of the house, so that all four rooms benefitted from their heat. The roof was of rived boards, and the walls were weather-boarded on the out-side. Soon after moving in John added an ell, creating two more rooms, so that there were four bedrooms in all, a large social room, and a dining area. There were also the smoke house, cook house, privy, slave cabins, barns, tack house and a few other out-buildings. It might not have compared to a Tidewater mansion, but for that part of the country in that time it was one of the finest resi-dences. I understand that the pear orchard had already been planted and that some fields were cleared and in clover when the family arrived. John set immediately to raising pigs, cows, and chickens, and fields of corn and dark tobacco.

All went extremely well for the first twelve years. The farm prospered beyond even John Bell's expectations. He was a respected farmer and businessman in the community and an elder in his church. His family in 1816 was his wife Lucy, and children Jesse, John, Jr., Drewry, Esther, Elizabeth, Richard Williams, and Joel Egbert. (His third son, Benjamin, had died in 1810. Your uncle Zadok had already taken up the law profession and settled in Alabama and, as you know, has died.) John owned eight Negro slaves of various ages. In that year, Richard Williams was only four and Joel Egbert three, while their father was sixty-six, clearly still potent in the early winter of his manhood. John had ever been forehanded and owed neither money nor favour to any one. Indeed, he was one of the wealthiest men for a day's ride in any direction. No man could have asked for more blessings.

And then what the Bells began to call "our family troubles" commenced. Once it was hard upon them, members of the family cast their minds backwards and recollected several portentous events they had at the time refused to believe to be anything but strange and unrelated.

The first involved a black beast with a huge head that John spotted sitting at the far end of one of his corn fields. Initially, he thought it was an enormous dog that had wandered into the region. As he and the beast continued to stare at each other unmoving for the better part of a minute John became convinced that it was no dog but rather some wild creature native to the still-untamed land. In those days, although the Indian menace was all but ended, settlers like John Bell who had lived there during their threat could not bring themselves to shed the habit of carrying a flintlock wherever they roved. Moreover, game was then so prevalent and so unused to man that it often approached within easy gunshot, making hunting unnecessary for those prepared.

John took careful aim at the beast and fired. When the

smoke cleared, he found it had disappeared. He reloaded and marched to the end of the field, but there was no mark of blood nor any sign of the animal.

A few weeks later, John spotted a gigantic bird on the farm, larger than a turkey. This time, the creature flew off before John could fire his weapon.

In this same season, Betsy was walking along the verge of the Bell woods, minding her younger brothers. All three saw a girl, about Betsy's age, hanging from a low branch of an oak tree, swinging back and forth. The girl wore a dress of pale green. When Betsy called a greeting to her, she made no reply. As the three Bell children drew closer she vanished. When Betsy told the mammy among the family slaves, Chloe pronounced that they had seen a witch, as "green be de color ob de Devil's hag." All these things happened within the space of several weeks, in the months of September and October of 1817.

It was in the first grip of winter, that is to say at Christmas of 1817, when the unnatural moved out of the fields and woods and up to the Bell home itself. It was first perceived as a knocking on the outer walls, upon the tightly closed shutters, and against the thick wood of the back door. Each time John Sr. would investigate, he found nothing. His guess was that, as this was the time just prior to the circuit court trial against him, Kate Batts had put one or more of her Negro slaves up to tormenting him.

Your grandmother Bell had always been a sound sleeper. After the first few incidents of the noises, she began to catch only light and fitful rest. Whenever the noises would start, she would spring from her bed and rush to the resounding back door only to find her husband already there with lighted candle and lifting the

21

The green-garbed apparition

wooden crossbar. At that instant, the noises would stop. Quick as John might be, not so much as a shadow was perceived skulking away into the night.

The noises continued through the winter, generally beginning at ten o'clock, some two hours after the youngest children had gone to sleep and an hour after the parents retired, and ending around midnight.

It was in January of 1818 that I had my first inkling something was amiss in the Bell household. Your mother, who in the first two years of my tuition had been ever bright-eyed and attentive, began arriving at the school house with dark circles under her eyes, her eyelids half lowered from lack of sleep. She stood at the writing bench staring at her penmanship exercises as if they were in Hebrew, and when she recited from the *New England Primer*, it was as if she were in a somnambulist's trance. When I required a reason her eyes grew wide with alarm, but she merely replied that "the house was making strange noises" and was keeping the family from its proper rest.

It was quite soon after questioning your mother that I had occasion to speak with John Bell about her condition. He had called together his closest friends, that is, Rev. Sugg Fort, James Johnston, and myself, to ride several miles with him to the home of Mr. James Byrns, who served part time as a lawyer and magistrate in that region and whom John had engaged to defend him in the court case. The plan was for all of us to put our heads together to defeat Kate Batts's claims.

As John and I rode saddle to saddle, some distance behind Rev. Fort and Mr. Johnston, I inquired of the strange noises being made by his house. He started as if he had been struck by lightning. He asked me exactly what Betsy had said, and I told him. At that, he seemed to relax somewhat. He assured me that it would only be a matter of time until he and his sons had isolated the noises (either loose boards being disturbed by the wind or else nesting squirrels he guessed), and then all would return to peace within the Bell household.

Later, at the Byrns home, the debate raged thick and hot about how John should be defended. John, however, who should have had the most to say, was curiously taciturn. Even more curious, when it came time for us all to move to the dining room for the meal Mrs. Byrns had prepared, John remained in the common room on his chair. He was formally given an invitation to the table not once but twice, and on each occasion shook his head and offered no words of explanation for his refusal. Although we kept our voices low, we could not help but remark among ourselves at John's behaviour. During the hour we had debated he had hardly spoken and seemed quite abstracted and dejected.

Almost immediately upon finishing the meal, on account of the hour, the quickly falling night, and the distance to our homes, we bade the Byrnses farewell. Again, John rode beside me. He asked what we had said at the table of his behaviour, and I told him. His hand went to his jaw, and he rubbed it as if he had recently taken a blow there.

"I was unable to help myself," he confided. "Even before we entered the house, I began to have a strange feeling inside my mouth. It was as if a fungus was suddenly growing along both sides of my tongue, so thick that it pressed against my teeth and jaws. Did you notice that my face looked swollen?"

I told him I had not.

"Well, it wasn't my imagination, I'll tell you. It filled my mouth so much that I could hardly speak. I certainly would not have been able to eat. I felt it was less impolite to decline the invitation to dinner entirely than to sit at their table and refuse their food. I have never been so embarrassed in my life."

I commiserated and suggested that it might have been brought on by John's upset over the law suit. If I had been similarly assaulted, I, too, might have been so outraged that I would have become tongue-tied.

"Perhaps," John answered, his face bleaker than the path we rode upon. "But tongue-tied and tongue-swollen are two different matters." He asked me to estimate the degree of the Byrnses' insult. I replied that husband and wife had appeared more confused than offended. "Well, there is nothing for me to do but ride back there tomorrow, explain what happened, and offer my apologies," he decided. And that is precisely what he did.

At the time, I had no idea that the cause of your grandfather's affliction had nothing to do with the law suit and everything to do with the "house noises." This was all I knew of the haunting (and indeed any one outside the Bell family knew) for quite a while, and I assure you I had no full understanding of the implications until much later.

As one who has lived in a log house, I will tell you that it is in the cold months when you find yourself most frequently sharing shelter with the tiny creatures of God's world, particularly the mice and the insects. Whatever had lurked outside the Bell home, however, behaved exactly the opposite, invading only after the winter winds turned mild. According to Betsy, it happened on a Sunday night in May, at the same hour that had brought the outside noises. Looking back across the years, I do not believe I have tricked myself in calculating that it was the Sunday directly following the incident with Kate Batts at Fort's meeting house.

This time, the noises sounded as if a rat had gotten into Richard and Joel's room and was gnawing on a footpost of their bed. They were awakened and cried out. Immediately, John Jr. and Drewry came across the hall, candles lit. The instant they opened the door, the noises stopped. Richard detailed the sounds and their supposed place of origin, but, upon close investigation, no chew marks were found. No sooner had the older boys left the room but the noises began again, only to stop the instant they were called back. Despite a tedious march back and forth until past midnight, neither rat nor evidence of rat could be found; nor could any chink be located in the room large enough to admit something as tiny as a mouse.

In the morning, the parents were told. That night the noises resumed but with more vigour. The boys tore their room apart, to no avail. During periods of investigation and with candles glowing, the noises stopped. As soon as darkness cloaked the house they began again, lasting usually until the witching hour had passed.

At the end of that week, again on a Sunday, the noises moved into Elizabeth's room. Again, no rational cause could be found. As I have related, there were four bedrooms in the house. John and Lucy slept on the ground floor, in the large room created by the adding of the ell. Upstairs, Betsy had the room directly above them. In the front, Richard and Joel shared a bed in the second upper bedroom, and John Jr. and Drewry slept together in the third. The arrangement had been somewhat tighter in previous years, until Esther married Alexander Bennett

Porter in July of 1817, leaving Elizabeth to sleep alone in one bedroom, and Jesse married Martha Gunn the following October, taking with him to his new home the bed that had crowded up next to that one holding John Jr. and Drewry.

Gradually, the invisible creature that had invaded the Bell home was growing stronger and bolder. Now covers began to slip slowly off the feet of the children's beds, as if a mischievous prank were being played. At the same time, the noises took on an animal-like quality. The children heard the smacking of lips and muffled, throaty sounds like someone choking or strangling. The visitations began to lengthen to as late as three o'clock. Then, added to the animate sounds, came noises of stones being dropped on the roof, of ducks flapping noisily out of a body of water, of a storm raging outside, of large dogs fighting in the yard, of trace chains or harness being dragged across the wooden floors, and furniture being moved. The noises were added like a child learning a repertoire of songs upon a tin flute he has been given, once possessed never to be abandoned. No physical evidence whatsoever could be found for the noises.

As the year 1818 wore on, the creature gained physical strength as well. What had been gentle but insistent tugs upon the bed clothes were now furious and swift strippings. Even the combined restraints of Drewry and John Jr. were no match to keep the covers off the floor.

Many stories had I heard purporting to be true of ghosts and spirits that have haunted houses, but never had I heard of one that physically assaulted the inhabitants. This being did.

On an October night in 1818, following a rare evening when the creature had declined to raise its ghostly rumpus, Betsy was awakened from sleep by the twisting of her hair. Panicked as she was by the knowledge that the being had finally dared to touch her person, she lay as still as possible, hoping it would go away. A moment later, she was being dragged out of her bed head first. Every hank of her hair felt as if it were being yanked out by the roots. She began to scream for help, then realized that the voices of Joel and Richard were raised in similar alarm. The thing was apparently capable of attacking two persons simultaneously, in two separate rooms, as it had grabbed Richard by the hair in the same instant.

This was the final proof to John and Lucy that they were not dealing with any earthly force but were rather enduring the waxing malevolence of a supernatural spirit. In the face of such knowledge, they knew that they could no longer endure the tormenting alone but had to enlist the outside succour of at least one other Christian family.

The Johnston clan were among the first settlers in the Red River area and a noble breed. Chief among John Bell's friends was James Johnston, who was about ten years John's junior. He and his wife, Rebecca Porter Johnston, had a passel of children and were the Bell family's closest neighbours, owning the property just to the east.

On November 5, John took Mr. and Mrs. Johnston into his confidence, swearing them to absolute silence regarding the frightening events.[5] Soon after, the couple came to spend the night. They ate supper with the Bells. Then James, who was a very religious man, produced his Bible and in the presence of the assembled Bell family (except for the two youngest boys, whom they feared would become even more deranged by the meeting and who had already been tucked into their bed) read various passages, such as that in First Samuel, where Saul uses the witch of Endor to call up Samuel from the dead and in the eighth chapter of Luke, where the apostle tells us that Jesus drove seven demons from Mary Magdalene. This James did to remind those gathered that such things truly inhabit the earth. Then he read from the first chapter of Mark, where Jesus encounters a man in the Capernaum synagogue possessed of an unclean spirit that spoke to him. Jesus answers, "Be silent and come out of him!" You know your Bible well enough to know that the spirit gave a loud cry and departed. James suggested that the assembled group imitate the Lord's actions. They all joined hands, prayed the Lord's Prayer, then said together, "Demon, in the name of Jesus Christ, be silent and go out of this house forever!" This they did three times. The house was ominously still. Mr. Johnston then launched into an eloquent and earnest prayer for the Bell family's deliverance from the unseen affliction.

Soon after, James and Rebecca retired to the upstairs bedroom closest to Betsy's, which had been vacated for their use. They did not have long to wait until the noises began and the covers were ripped from their bed. The Johnstons had not witnessed the slow building of the thing's strength as the Bells had, so that their first exposure to its pranks was at full fury. Consequently, they were mightily affrighted and had all they could do not to run screaming back across the dark fields to their own home. As James told it to me later, they were treated to the spirit's entire repertoire — gnawed bedposts, thumping roof, cat wailings, sounds of furniture moving. Each time he would light the candle, the noises would stop, only to move to another bedroom. The moment he and his wife lay again in silence, the spirit was back.

Towards midnight, the thing began its sounds of laboured swallowing and smacking lips. This led Mr. Johnston to conclude that the thing had human qualities and perhaps also possessed human understanding. At this, he cried out, "In the name of Jesus, who or what are you? What is it that you want?" The room grew suddenly silent, as if the Lord's name had frightened the thing off. Eventually, enough time passed that the Johnstons actually hoped they had chased the thing away forever. Within a few more minutes, owing to the late hour and their exhaustion of mind caused by the noises and bedclothes antics, both Johnstons were drifting towards sleep. It was at this moment that their room reverberated with fierce laughter, starting them straight up in the darkness.

The covers were whipped off the bed, and the creature traveled from room to room like a whirlwind, exposing every person in the house to the night cold, snarling as it did. Eventually, it stopped in Elizabeth's room and settled on a great tugging match, using her hair as the rope. Betsy struggled fiercely. Just as the elders entered the room with their lights, the clear sound of a hand smacking flesh was heard, and Betsy's face snapped to the side from an invisible blow. Her jaw dropped in surprise. Mrs. Johnston expected that Betsy would have burst into tears, but so plucky was your mother that she refused to give the thing such satisfaction. For her stubbornness she was slapped six or seven times more. Soon, both her cheeks glowed red. Still, she refused to shed a tear, although she could not resist crying out in pain as she was physically dragged around the room by the hair of her crown.

"Cease this at once!" Mr. Johnston cried out.

Betsy's head thumped lightly to the floor as the thing let go her hair.

"You see?" said Mr. Johnston to the elder Bells. "It has intelligence and understands the meaning of my words."

"Then it is a demon indeed," John concluded. "What can we do?"

The invisible spirit began panting and making its choking noises.

James helped Betsy up from the floor and wrapped his arms protectively around her. "You must abandon your pact to keep this evil habitation a secret and call upon the help of all your neighbours. Surely, the thoughts and prayers of a communion of Christians is more than enough even for such a spirit."

With that, the creature offered up a barnyard full of noises and yanked the bedding so violently from the frame that the tick ripped open. Goose feathers flew in a storm around the room. Then the lower tick, filled with corn shucks, began bouncing up and down upon the hide strips that held it off the floor.

"You are right, Brother Johnston," John said. "We can no longer endure this torture alone."

I was among the half dozen friends enlightened on the following day, which was November 6. After listening dumbfounded to John's detailed account, the first question that sprang to my lips was why he had kept secret for so long such a terrible visitation. John's reply was immediate and complex, convincing me that he had already asked himself the same question many times. At first he had just hoped it was malicious mischief that would stop when the trial was over; then he had blamed the noises on shifting earth, as the ground under the Bell house was honeycombed with cave chambers.[6] He declared that the community had been troubled enough with Bell business over the trial and John's banishment from the church. The last thing he wanted was for his neighbours to believe the Bell family was making up troubles to get sympathy. Finally, he didn't want his farm and family to become the curiosity of the land, the place where something unnatural or even supernatural [was] happening.

I had my own theory about why John Bell had sworn his family to silence, despite the obvious strain it was exacting upon them: John had already been characterized by court and church alike as a less than Christian man. If the Red River community found out that a wicked spirit lived within his walls, might they not wonder if he had gone completely over to the other side and used unholy rituals to call up the demon himself?

Fortunately, none of John's friends was so backward or superstitious. We all came to the family's aid with generous hearts, willing to do whatever might be necessary to restore the Bell home to peace. Unfortunately, the invisible spirit would not cooperate. Enlisted to their neighbours' aid was virtually the entire community, and I shall name them here once, in case you should need to consult with the main players in this more-than-Greek tragedy. Directly after the James Johnstons were informed, so were myself, the John Johnstons, the Carneys, Norfleets, Northingtons, Frank Miles and his brothers, Elder Reuben Ross, the Suggs, and the Rev. Sugg Fort along with the teeming Fort clan. Soon after, the word traveled as ripples from a disturbed pond to the Revs. Thomas and James Gunn, the Gooches, Gardners, Dardens, and Bartletts. Eventually, offering their aid were the Pitmans,

Longs, Ruffins, Mathewses, the Ayerses, Morrises, Herrings, Wimberleys, Chesters, Bournes, McGowens, Gorhams, Waterses, and Roysters.

While I believe I possess a better memory than most and while the details of such a phenomenal event as this would naturally linger in the mind better than quotidian events of the past, I do not recount these many good families by heart. From the day I was taken into the Bell family's confidence I kept a log of all that I witnessed and all that was related to me of the spirit and its doings. I do not call the notes I made a diary, since that word connotes a daily recording and, moreover, a concentration on personal experiences. Neither of these is true. What is true is that I realized early on that the Bell family troubles were of such a unique nature that they merited a log, kept in as detached a manner as possible. I will also admit here that I have long admired authors and chroniclers and thought that this subject might provide an excellent theme for me once it had come to its conclusion. As you must now realize, both mother and the rest of the Bell family have been adamant about keeping these events shrouded in darkness. Once I joined myself to them in marriage, I gave up all aspirations of publishing my observations. Owing to the scarcity of paper, at the time I made only notes of dates, places, persons involved, and events, all be it including even the superstitions and lies arising around it. This is my third setting down of the tale (the first one quite brief and the second not much longer, due to my erroneous anticipation of imminent death), and it is as complete as notes and memory together allow. I have omitted nothing, and even though this made for an arduous task I have done so for two reasons. First, I have no way of knowing what might be an important clew towards your mother's salvation. Secondly, I know that should you decide to release this to the greater world, the scientific community will want to have every fact recorded for study and comparison, should a similar event arise.

Enough apology.

Once Rev. Sugg Fort had heard the descriptions of the disturbances, he became convinced of the "Batts theory." That is, he thought that Kate Batts had sent one or more of her Negro servants over nightly to give the Bells a scare and keep them from sleep. When the trial began, John would surely look so haggard and distressed that the judge would instantly believe him suffering under the weight of certain guilt. Sugg suggested that the method of torture was through the roof, that holes had been found or bored in during the period that noises were heard outside. Later, wires with fish hooks were let down onto the covers, so that they could be whisked from the beds. The stinging attacks upon Betsy's face, he opined, were dried peas shot down through hollow reeds, as children are wont to employ in worrying each other and their pets. As additional proof, he reminded us that all the attacks had occurred in the upper bedrooms. As soon as a candle was ignited, the Negroes would desist, crawl along the roof to another room, and begin playing tricks there. Finally, he put forth the theory that the family had never been able to spot the noise makers outside because they were darkies in dark clothing upon a dark roof and that the feeble light of candles was not enough to pierce such a great distance upward to their hiding place.

Several among the group liked Rev. Fort's postulations. We got a ladder and examined the roof, in daylight and by night. We found no holes; nor could we perceive openings through the bedroom ceilings. Samuel Northington, who had journeyed with John and Lucy to Red River from North Carolina, asked if any fishing hooks or dried peas had ever been found in the thoroughly examined bedrooms. Being quite loyal to Sugg, John Bell commissioned his boys to scour again the rooms before any one could answer in the negative. After the course of two hours' diligent but vain searching, the Reverend withdrew his theory.

Mr. Northington, who must have felt obliged to advance another theory after barking Rev. Fort's so neatly out of the tree, suggested that perhaps all the noises, tremors, and dislocation of objects had resulted from minor earthquakes under the Bell home. Ever since 1811, when the earthquakes centered on New Madrid had changed the course of rivers and created an entire new lake, the settlers of the area had been mighty leery of the fundament of their new land. Many had hypothesized the Lord's anger at their having stolen the area away from the savage red man and that even greater doom awaited the white dispossessors. So great was the fear of divine retribution struck in the common man that camp meetings reached a zenith of attendance. But now, six years after the final tremors had subsided, most had all but forgotten and lapsed to moderate worship of the Almighty.

I was the one who reminded Mr. Northington that no earthquake could drag Elizabeth Bell around a room by her hair, nor smack her face crimson. Further, I reminded him that the school house lay not a quarter mile away and that I had felt not the slightest motion of the earth in all the past months.

Rough and homespun as the group might have been, we all counted ourselves men and women of an enlightened age. We struggled mightily to put our minds to natural explanations and, in so doing, we failed mightily. As if to discourage our efforts, the cause of the uproar had remained perversely quiet. In the nights directly following the visit of Mr. and Mrs. Johnston, several of us took turns sleeping upstairs with the Bell children, and all we heard was the fleeting noise of trace harness, dogs barking, or the faintest puff of a breeze that should not have been there. It was just enough to worry those of us who had never experienced that which we had been told existed, and just too little for us to believe the litany of the Bell family's fantastic statements.

My second overnight stay, on Saturday, November 14, left me alone with Lucy Bell for a few minutes before we were to retire. Your grandmother was then forty-eight years old and looked older. She must have been a handsome woman in her youth, but much of her vitality had been drained by the moving to such an uncivilized place, by wresting a living out of the land with hardly any conveniences, and by the bearing and rearing of eight children. Now she was thinner and more care-worn than I had ever known her, such were the privations dealt to her by the unseen demon. I shared with her then my premonition of months before that something was amiss when her daughter had come to school so bleary-eyed and weary.

"You care for her beyond the normal concern of a teacher for a pupil," your grandmother said to me with confidence.

I felt a great heat come upon my face. "I do," I admitted. "She is turning into a woman before my eyes. Surely you are aware that no one for a day's ride in any direction is as comely as your daughter, Mrs. Bell." At this time, your mother, although only thirteen, had a finely turned woman's figure. This coupled with the angelic countenance she had always owned, her huge blue eyes, her creamy-white complection and her wealth of golden hair made her a goddess among the common folk of Red River.

"But I have endeavoured to keep my feelings locked in my heart," I hastened to add, "since I have never entertained the hope that my tender feelings could be requited."

"And why not?" Lucy asked, thoroughly surprising me, as she had never before hinted that she harboured connubial thoughts concerning myself and her younger daughter.

When I could find my tongue, I answered, "For one reason, I am too old for Elizabeth. She is only thirteen, and I am halfway to my thirty-first year. I am more than twice her age."

"When I married Mr. Bell," Lucy said calmly, "I was but twelve, and he was thirty-two. Moreover, it is curious that you call my daughter the most comely creature for a day's ride in any direction, for everyone in Red River believes the same to be true of our 'Bachelor Teacher.' Do not blush, Dick Powell. You are by far the most learned among us. More importantly, you have uncommon common sense. What is more, the heart that holds such secret tenderness for my daughter is a noble one. No man merits nor holds greater respect in our community. I could ask no better match for Elizabeth, considering it is plain that you love her."

"But she does not love me," I protested. "Betsy has her eye on a lad of no small beauty: Joshua Gardner. He is seventeen or eighteen, of good family, and all but prepared to begin a family himself. What is more, he loves her as well."

"We like Joshua very much," Lucy affirmed, "but we also like you, Dick. Elizabeth knows this. If you dare compete for her favours, you will find no opposition here."

Hardly had her daughter's name passed Lucy's lips than Betsy began screaming upstairs. Together, we rushed up in response. You must understand that, to this point, I had seen nothing unnatural or fearsome enough to convince me of the tale of the Bell family troubles. Within a space of moments, all my doubts were forever dispelled.

The door to Betsy's room was difficult to open. Once I had forced myself inside, I realized that the bed clothes had been piled against the door and the bed was stripped. Betsy sat alone on the center of the tick, wearing only a night dress. She had her arms raised to her face, as if to ward off an attacker. Suddenly, her right arm flung away to the extreme and her head jerked to the left. The sound of her flesh being struck was unmistakable. In the light of my candle I could see that her cheeks were already aflame from the spirit's attack.

Lucy rushed past me, pushed Betsy against the head board and positioned herself so that the invisible demon would have to move her first before attacking her daughter again. You cannot imagine my pain at being utterly helpless to protect your mother. I felt it improper enough to be in her bedroom, yet there I was not only staring at her in her undress but also completely at a loss of what to do in her defense.

The room became suddenly as still as a tomb. By this time, John, John Jr., and Drewry were beside me, but no one uttered a sound. We were like an audience hushed before a great theatrical performance. Then, from out of the silence came the revolting noise of someone hawking phlegm from his throat, immediately followed by the sound of spitting. My candle winked out. The act was repeated twice more, extinguishing the candles of John and John Jr., until the lot of us stood in near-total darkness.

The creature gave out a burst of wild laughter and was gone. In the next few nights, the thing offered divers exhibitions to all the neighbours who chose to share the Bell roof. The show varied as to specifics, but never was Betsy spared. We feared so much for her safety that the committee settled upon the idea of moving her to the homes of close friends. In the course of three weeks she slept in the beds of her boon and brave companions Rebecca Porter (the niece of Rebecca Porter Johnston) and Partheny Thorn (nicknamed Theny), with her married sister Esther, with sister-in-law Martha, and also at the homes of John and James Johnston. In each and every case, the creature followed her and meted out physical punishment, although we were slightly comforted by the fact that it was always of brief duration and of less severity than she had experienced at home.

The Bells were asked if, whenever Betsy was away, they were spared the creature's torment. They assured us that the thing's antics continued unabated. On these nights, however, none of the neighbours had been invited into the Bell home.

Enough time had now passed for many in the immediate community to have experienced first-hand the unnatural goings on. Theories abounded. As a bachelor and living by myself, I was seldom privy to these conversations. I had one prolonged opportunity, however, to hear the accumulated opinions when I traveled down to Nashville at the end of November with several men. Harvesting had been completed, which allowed the time for the journey, and no later date could be risked as heavy snows had been known to fall in early December. The farmers in the group went mostly to pick up crafted furniture they had ordered from Baltimore and Philadelphia. I took the holiday both as a helping hand and to see if I could augment my pitiful library.

Those I traveled with were neighbours of the Bells but of varying sentiments towards them. Horatio Sory and Rev. Ambrose Bourne were neither physically nor emotionally close to the family and had yet to visit the farm since word had spread of the evil habitation (although Rev. Bourne would eventually become close and a believer); George Wimberley had visited, heard noises only, and was skeptical; Richard Carney had seen Betsy punished, had been a long believer of demonic possession, and was their staunch defender. Therefore, the arguments took on a gritty nature. The most popular notion amongst the community was that Elizabeth Bell was perpetrating a hoax. For what reason the group could not divine. That it was so, Sory and Wimberley were more certain. For one thing, they argued, your mother was always inside the Bell house when the noises and other disturbances had occurred. For another, except for one isolated assault on Richard in total darkness, she was the only person who had been attacked. While we were seated together before the camp fire, Mr. Sory whipped his head back and forth, cried out, and threw himself to the ground, to demonstrate how such an attack could be feigned.

I attempted to remain as calm as possible and reminded the group about the discolorations on Betsy's cheeks.

"How can such marks be counterfeited?" I asked.

"They are simply the colour of extreme exertion," Mr. Sory answered. "And if she is demented, perhaps she has indeed convinced herself that she is being attacked. The crippled of mind are capable of many amazing feats. Remember the tremendous strength of one that Jesus dealt with. Her mind may be ordering her blood to rise hotly to her cheeks, just as yours is doing now, Dick."

All the men laughed at the flush that had come over me. I realized then that my feelings towards your mother were not as hidden as I had supposed. I had been tacitly elected by the group as her defender.

"Is it not strange that this creature follows Elizabeth and Elizabeth alone from the Bell house?" Rev. Bourne asked.

"Yes, it is," I granted. "But, whenever that happens, it is at the same time tormenting the rest of the family at home."

"We have only their word on that," Rev. Bourne pointed out.

"Then you must visit their house when Elizabeth is away, to prove to the skeptical among the community that the family does indeed tell the truth," I said.

"I shall," he answered. In December he did as he had promised, and that was the beginning of his conversion.

"As to the sounds of choking, sobbing, and spitting," said Horatio Sory, "I myself have seen a man who could cast his voice across a space without moving his lips. He could, in fact, utter entire sentences. It seemed by my lights very unworldly, but he assured us it was quite natural. Perhaps Elizabeth has acquired this talent as well."

"But for what purpose?" I asked, for perhaps the tenth time. That question was the one that ever silenced the group.

"I think we do Elizabeth and her parents a grave disservice," Richard Carney said, staring into the fire. "I say we are looking in the wrong direction. There is one person among us in Red River who has openly cursed the Bells: Old Kate Batts. You heard the words yourself last spring, Dick, at Fort's meeting house."

I could not deny the malediction Kate Batts had placed on the Bell family: "You may have your broad acres as well as mine, purchased at a penitence. You may have your big house and your salubricated health right now. But just wait and see what sad changes shall soon descend upon you. And more than you."

"You heard her words, and so did others," Mr. Carney went on. "This business began before she got her judgement against John. I say she conjured up a spell against him and his family, and it got beyond her powers. She may be satisfied as to the hell it has raised already, but I think she's powerless to send it back to where it came from. Stupid old woman. What we have amongst us, and I mean all of us since this is the concern of every Christian family in Red River, is a witch. Kate Batts's witch. And until we acknowledge it to be what it is, we'll have no chance of getting rid of it."

If I had been able to produce a temporary silence with my words, Richard Carney stretched a pall over the group with his. This was not the first time he had promoted the idea; nor was he the sole owner of it.

By the time we arrived back in Red River from Nashville, a considerable portion of the community were shunning Kate Batts. The wives suddenly had no time to listen to her prattle. There was never extra wool nor flax to be found for her slaves, and there were certainly no spare pins to share. Even the store keepers in Port Royal began asking her to make immediate payment on the credit they had extended.

Although she might indeed have had some "things flying around loose in her belfry," Kate Batts was not stupid. She understood quickly the reason for her ostracism, and, true to her form, answered it on the attack. From her point of view, the Bells had invented demonic tormentation after she spoke her angry words at Fort's meeting house. Their united act was done, she protested, precisely to isolate her from the rest of the community. This she told to any one within ear shot, but few were willing to listen. As Wm. Shakespear [sic] has written, she was truly "hoisted on her own petard." And so the spirit became generally known as "Kate Batts's witch," "Old Kate," or sometimes "The Bell's witch." As the phrases came into common usage, I marveled as to how little we had advanced since the days of Cotton Mather and the Salem witch trials. In later months and upon reflection, I realized that Red River's witch obsession was not just a legacy of New England; many of our settlers had either come directly from England and Scotland or else were the children of emigrants. They had had their dread training in witchcraft under the rule of the likes of James VI. Their superstitious beliefs were to be of little use to them, however, for this creature was as much like an old hag woman as a cannon ball is to an arrow.

Shortly after we returned, the Bells did indeed prove that the entity could bedevil Betsy in a friend's home whilst, in the same night, it continued to wreck havoc at the Bell house. Moreover, Betsy could be sent off to her

43

own bed with a friend (which is what she constantly pleaded for), and family and friends would continue to question the spirit below in the social room.

The main diversion of guests during the last days of 1818 was to question the "witch," in order to gain a better fix on what it was. This was done by asking such interrogatives as could be answered with knocks upon the walls or furniture. Counting questions provided the clearest responses. It would be asked how many people were present in the room, how many rooms in the house, how many chairs, and so forth, and it always answered correctly. The disconcerting part was that sometimes the responses were not merely sharp rappings but in smacking of lips or the sound of claws being raked along wood. There was no doubt that we had exposed a rational mind. After hearing the sounds of claws, however, many of us were not anxious to learn its unseen shape. Its power, moreover, seemed ever to increase. Now, whenever any one insulted it or attempted to keep the covers on their beds, it reacted with swift and stinging blows to their faces. Only occasionally did this happen to visitors and never to me. Betsy, Richard Williams, Drewry, and Joel suffered the preponderancy of its violent nature.

Fascinated as I was by this mystery, I resisted the temptation to use my proximity to the Bell house as an excuse to make of myself a pest. In the first three months after learning of the haunting I visited only four times. On my fourth call I posed several questions to the thing, using Latin and the little I knew of Greek. Its noises ceased each time for long periods, and for once it did not respond with the correct number of knocks. I was somewhat relieved to learn that it did not possess classical knowledge. In the back of my mind, I had envisioned this creature as one of the fallen angels, by which I mean something truly Satanic in nature. A demon more local and less ancient seemed to me less formidable.

A few persons credited my questioning in dead languages with giving the creature voice. To their way of thinking, I had so challenged its intelligence that it was compelled by pride to speak. It is clear now, however, that it was simply the proper time, as it had first been the spirit's time to make noises outside, then inside, next to move objects, then to attack persons. What had arrived at the Bell home was growing and evolving, just as the Bell children were.

I have already mentioned its human-like noises of smacking lips, swallowing, choking, and of moanings. At the turn of 1819, it began giving forth whispers, like a rustling of birch leaves. In the first weeks they were so soft that people argued amongst themselves as to whether or not there were words concealed within. Then, one evening in the last week of January, when the James Johnstons had again volunteered to share the Bells' roof, the thing enlisted all the practice it had made at producing sound and spoke. I was not present, but Mr. Johnston pronounced it more marvelous and terrible than anything he had known in his entire life.

Although the words were feeble and hollow-sounding, they were the passages James Johnston had selected from the Bible on the night he and his wife had first been invited to help deal with the manifestation. No sooner had the passages of demoniac possession been recited than it went straight through the Lord's Prayer and concluded with the words, "Demon, in the name of Jesus Christ, be silent and go out of this house forever!" As if it were not enough for the thing to have duplicated every syllable

45

spoken by Mr. Johnston at that prayer session, it was also clear, the softness of the words notwithstanding, that it was speaking in an excellent likeness of James's voice as well.

And then it switched to a feminine voice and ended with one more sentence: "Well said, Old Sugar Mouth."

No one had any doubt as to the sincerity of Mr. Johnston's pious Methodist nature. That he knew his Bible and was quite proud of quoting it with his rich baritone voice there was also no doubt. In one fell incident, the Bells learned that the creature was indeed intelligent, had the power of speech, possessed a prodigious memory, and enjoyed a barbed sense of humour. Ever after that, when it would address James Johnston, it never called him anything but "Old Sugar Mouth."[7]

If the fame of "Kate Batts's witch" had been cast abroad in the months before, it was nothing compared to the excitement that spread after news went out about the entity finding a tongue. In the days that followed its first words many questions were put to it, but it did not answer directly. Rather, amongst the low and often indistinct sounds, people heard or thought they heard passages from the Good Book being recited. Then, one night, John Jr. addressed the creature for the first time. From your personal acquaintance with your uncle, you know him to be a fine thinker, one given to pondering privately until he is ready to share ideas. He had been hanging back for long months, merely watching and listening, refusing to become impassioned by the creature's displays.

"Who are you and what do you want?" John Jr. asked.

Although I was not present, I understand the room became totally silent in anticipation.

"I am the spirit of someone who was once happy and who has been disturbed," it said in a tiny whisper.

"You were a living person?" John continued.

"Yes."

"Who were you?"

The expected reply did not come.

"Who or what has disturbed you?" John asked, several times. Despite much persistence and patience, the thing was not heard again that night; nor did it launch into any of its physical tricks. This gave hope to the Bells that once the spirit could tell them precisely what had drawn it to the farm it would eventually return to rest. Their hope was in vain.

Even as the creature found a voice, its torments upon your mother reached a new height. It combined its voice with physical attacks upon her person. Theny Thorn was one of Betsy's closest companions and was quite willing to sleep in her bedroom, as the "witch" seemed to have an aversion to the older girl. Perhaps it was because Theny was a chatter box. She was also no match for Betsy in terms of wits. Theny had heard that a four leaf clover kept on one's person would make a witch visible. She and her mother had paid a visit to friends in a near part of Kentucky, and there she had chanced upon such a stem of clover. According to her, she stuck it into a pocket, forgot about it, and carried it home. The next time she came to overnight at the Bell house she wore the dress. She had still forgotten about the leaf, and she swore that she had told Betsy nothing of it, but the "witch" was aware of it just the same. It mocked Theny for believing such a foolish superstition and informed her that Betsy would be the one to pay for it. With that, Betsy fell backwards heavily upon her bed. Both her feet went into the air, and her shoes, although tightly laced, flew off her feet and hit the opposite wall. The next moment, the tucking combs she had placed in her hair to hold its wealth off her shoulders also went flying. The combs were of tortoise shell and very liable to damage, but they were not broken. These two acts were now added to the spirit's repertoire. For good measure, Betsy was again boxed about the face, and an unseen hand was clapped over her mouth, so that she could only breathe through her nose.

Whilst all this was happening, I continued to teach Betsy. I should say I taught her whenever she came to the school house, since she was often too sleepy or too sore to benefit from tutelage. Many nights I lay awake, pondering her unique relationship to the unseen entity. Your mother had been pestered by too many other persons about whether she was creating the thing or about theories of why it followed and attacked her. I saw no reason why I might be able to get any secret knowledge from her when her best friends and family had been unable. Instead, when the other pupils were all doing chores for me after the lessons, I took her aside and asked if she knew of anything I could do to make the spirit go away or at least to lessen the severity of its attacks on her. She simply cast her eyes downwards and gravely shook her head. I had never felt so frustrated or impotent.

Through these many trials, John and Lucy Bell endeavoured to keep their two smallest boys out of the fray as much as possible. Drewry, although older, seemed the most unnerved by the creature's antics. John Jr., as I have said, rightly assessed early on that he had virtually no power over the invisible, incorporeal spirit. He had a close friend, however, named Frank Miles, who took much convincing.

48

Betsy Bell, shown with shoe and tucking combs removed—
typical tricks of the Bell Witch

Frank was the strongest man in the community. I would judge him to have been six foot two inches tall, no less than 250 pounds and not a bit of it fat. No one could best him at arm wrestling; to do so would have been to risk your bones. He could hoist a log weighing as much as himself over his shoulder and carry it a quarter mile without once setting it down. It was said, although I never saw it, that his jaws were so strong he could crack a black walnut shell between his teeth.

Mr. Miles was not one of the community's most celebrated thinkers; manly, brute force was his answer to most any problem. Despite his good intentions, he was often violent when opposed, either by animate or inanimate objects. I thought him quite the show off and braggart as well. Added to this, his vocabulary was limited to simple oaths and phrases, many of these of the crudest origin. By that I mean he used many swear words, and he used them often. So facile was he at their employment that they occasionally slipped out while he was in a temper and women were near by. He would quickly apologize, but his apologies were hardly sincere, as it happened with regularity. Nor were many men keen on reminding him of his crudity, as he would find a way, under the guise of sport, to punch them hard in the shoulders or slap them forcefully on the backs soon after. All this being said, he nevertheless had at the bottom of it a good and loyal heart.

Frank counted himself not merely the best friend of John Jr. but also like an older brother to Betsy. As soon as he learned of the spirit's personal attacks on your mother, he took himself over to the Bell house with the stated purpose of wrestling the creature to a standstill.

But, just as Jacob found in wrestling with the Lord's angel, he could not overcome it.

"I was wondering when this great bumpkin would rush to poor Betsy's aid," the creature mocked, in the presence of several persons.

"Show yourself, coward," Frank shouted, "and I will punch you back to Perdition."

Betsy pleaded with Frank to desist, for she knew by much experience who would soon bear the brunt of the pain for Frank's effrontery.

"If it can hit you, then I can hit it," Frank reasoned.

"Do you think so?" the voice asked. With that, Betsy's head spun sideways from a fiercely delivered blow. As she cried out with the pain, Frank leapt across the room and threw himself upon the place directly in front of her, his bear like arms swinging inward to clutch the spirit. Finding nothing but thin air, he fell clumsily to the floor. The spirit laughed uproariously and pushed Betsy onto him.

A moment later, one of the social room chairs began to rock.

"Here I am," the creature said.

Frank rushed to the bait, again finding nothing but air, and breaking one of the chair legs as he crashed upon it. Any prudent man might have realized the futility of his actions at this point and desisted, but Frank staggered around the room after the voice, throwing himself this way and that, until even his great stamina was exhausted.

On another night, he volunteered to stay upstairs on guard. A bed was placed in the wide hallway for him, just outside of Betsy's room. As all the others before had experienced, toward midnight his covers started creeping

51

to the foot of the bed. Frank wrapped his hands around their tops and tugged with all his might. When light was finally brought upon the scene, the covers were found to be badly ripped. Frank was discovered upon the floor, underneath the ticking and the overturned bed frame.

On a third occasion, Frank strained his mental abilities to the fullest and brought with him a small sack of flour. When the spirit began talking, he would throw a hand full of the powder into the place from which the voice emanated, hoping to reveal its shape. "Kate" was only too willing to provide targets, until Lucy tired of having her room dusted and took the sack from Frank. Eventually, John Jr. banged it into Frank's brain that his efforts were only inciting the spirit to reprisals against Betsy. Thereafter, Frank gnashed his teeth much and cursed under his breath when hearing the thing or watching its antics, but he generally controlled his wrathy temper.

All the while, John Jr. coolly kept his own counsel, tucking the various clews inside his head until some positive action might come to him. When the first days of spring arrived, he announced that it was time for him to journey back to North Carolina, to represent the family in the settling of an estate on your grandfather Bell's side. I was present on this occasion, as were the entire Bell family and a few other of the neighbours. John's journey was being debated, for many reasons. Even though the year was 1819 and Tennessee had come a long way toward settlement, there were numerous dangers attached to travel back over the Appalachians, Indians and road pirates being two of them. Spring would be fully past before John could hope to return, depriving his father of his useful hand in running the farm. Further, the Bells had had only one message on the estate, and so could not know in what degree of settlement it was.

John argued that precisely their distance and blindness in the matter of the settlement demanded a representative for his father, that it was better for him to miss a few weeks of the farm's spring activities than during the busy summer. Finally, he felt he was serving no good in the matter of the "witch" and wished to relinquish his side of the bed to the many curious and solicitous neighbours who thought they might be of help. His last argument certainly held water. Since the creature had begun speaking, there never seemed to be less than two outsiders staying at the house.

Suddenly, the now-familiar feminine voice spoke up from the center of the room.

"Stay here, Brother John," it coaxed. "If you go, you will have made a long, hard journey for nothing." For the first time, the words were no longer breathy but full of voice, just as powerful as any one else in the group had been.

"And why is that?" John Jr. asked.

"Because the estate is entangled in legal difficulties and challenges. It will not be settled this year. You will spend much to travel and arrive back home with less in your pouch than when you left."

The younger John smirked at the intelligence. "How can you know this?"

"Oh, I know."

"You know nothing but how to torture this family. You are unwanted, and your words cannot be trusted."

"I have never lied to you," it said, with hurt in its tone.

"You have hardly ever spoken to me, since I have no desire to speak with you."

"Then go! Wear the shoes from your horse's hooves! But before you make your final decision, know this: whilst you are gone from this place, a young woman shall visit. She will be fair of face and might feel a strong pulsation toward you. A proper and well-bred young woman from Virginia she is. Not like the local sows who wriggle their nether parts at you now."

The ladies gasped at the rude words, spoken by a voice as high pitched and lilting as their own. John Jr. merely laughed.

"And what would be the business of such a refined woman out here?"

"That I will not tell you. But I will say that she holds a dowry of forty strapping Negroes, of porcelain from the Orient, of imported mahogany furniture. Marrying her would make you a king in a trice."

"The wind knows more than you," young John said, rising from his chair and leaving the house.

On the following day, which was Monday, March 29, John Jr. set out on his journey. I will not keep you hanging on tenter's hooks about the matter: he returned not less than six months later, empty handed. The estate was indeed entangled in law suits. Furthermore, there did come to Port Royal a young woman who, although not as fair of face as the "witch" might have described, was indeed from Virginia and who did indeed dress and carry herself as if she had forty Negroes in her dowry. John was never to meet her.

Enough familiarity with a thing, be it even a creature from Hell, will make one forget one's fears of it. Because the spirit possessed a feminine voice, because it had a playful side, and because it usually spoke the truth, those who visited the Bell house often found themselves relaxing around the "witch," despite the fact that it appeared to be of another plane. Most guilty of this were Bennett Porter and John Johnston, who would share gossip with it and laugh openly at its sharp words and antics. On occasion, even I found myself lowering my guard. Those like Betsy, who had felt its wrath, however, never made this mistake. In fact, as it grew in articulation and charm, it seemed to need to draw extra strength from the young woman.

On the night of March 29, not many hours after John Jr.'s departure for North Carolina, Betsy experienced her first "fit." This was to happen for months afterward with regularity, shortly before the spirit's normal evening appearance. Of a sudden, Betsy would fall into a faint. Upon the first incidents, she was immediately carried up to her bed. Later, she was allowed to lie comfortably on the floor where she had fallen, as we perceived that the more efforts we made to rouse her from her affliction, the more violent and prolonged it became. Once she was down, she would begin to take her breaths in high, panting gasps. She would indicate that she felt as if she were smothering, and indeed, she would soon pass out from lack of air. Her pupils would roll up under her upper lids, and her pulse could barely be felt. After a few minutes, she would revive, only to relapse. While she was awake, her eyes would grow huge with fear, and she would roll from side to side and appear to be struggling under the weight of a large, invisible mass. After a few weeks, we began to understand that she would not die from the attacks. They never lasted less than twenty minutes nor more than forty. Miraculously, no matter how much she struggled and seemed to suffer, she would be restored to perfect health, no worse for the wear, within ten minutes of awakening.

Shortly after a fit occurred was when the "witch" would appear, having apparently drawn its strength or nourishment from the poor girl. Never once while Betsy was in the throes of her fits did it give voice or perform any physical act. This, of course, led people to suspect afresh that Betsy and the "witch" were one and the same. Yet, as if to prove once and for all that such a notion was impossible, the spirit revealed even greater powers, which I shall illumine at the proper time.

On April 3 of 1819, remembering the success John Jr. had had with his question "Who are you and what do you want?" Rev. Sugg Fort again posed it.

And once again came the reply, although this time much stronger: "I am the spirit of someone who was once happy and who was disturbed."

"In what way were you disturbed, and what makes you unhappy now?" Rev. Fort asked.

"I am the spirit of a person who was killed close by here and buried. My grave has been disturbed. My bones have been dug up and scattered. One of my teeth was lost under this very house, and I am here to recover it."

With that, a noisy discussion ensued, concerning an incident that had taken place shortly before I had arrived. The Red River area was a place used as hunting ground by both the Chickasaw and Cherokee, although neither nation had towns in central Tennessee. Evidently, the land was so fiercely disputed that neither side could keep a hold on it.[8] Another kind of red man had inhabited the area many hundreds of years earlier, the proof of their habitation being mounds that they left behind, wherein they buried their dead.9

Such a mound had been found in woods on the Bell property when more land was being cleared for crops. As little more than bones, pottery, and arrowheads were ever found in the mounds, most farmers left these places sacred. Such was John Bell's plan. Soon after the area was cleared, however, Drewry Bell told another youth of the area named Corban Hall about the find. Being as thoughtless as any other boys their age, these two intended high adventure rather than disrespect. So it was that they opened the grave and scattered around various bones. During their sport, a jawbone separated from one of the skulls. Corban carried it away with him and into the Bell house. He and Drewry were sitting in the hallway discussing their disappointment over treasures not found. To demonstrate his feelings, Corban flung the jawbone against the far wall. One of the teeth came loose from its socket and dropped through a knothole in a floor board.

Just at that moment, John entered the house. When he received answer about the jawbone, he rebuked the boys sharply. The jaw he sent back with his right-hand servant, Dean, who replaced it and all the other scattered bones and attempted to restore the mound as much as possible to its original condition.

The entire family and several neighbours were aware of the incident. The party present during the voice's revelation moved as a body to the hallway. There in the floor, still unplugged, was the knothole. John decided that there was nothing to be done but to tear up that board and those adjoining it. When the ground beneath was exposed, to everyone's wonderment, no tooth could be found. All loose dirt was scraped into a pile and sifted, but still no tooth was found.

"The witch has spirited it away herself," Rev. Fort decided.

"I did no such thing," its voice answered from behind him. "But I did lie about being that Indian!" it crowed.

"Why would you do that?" Rev. Fort demanded.

"Why? To get Old Jack, of course. And I did get you, Jack, didn't I?" John was only called "Jack" by your grandmother Lucy, and it seemed a peculiar familiarity to those assembled, even for the "witch." John refused to dignify the question with an answer, although his eyes flashed and the muscles of his jaw stood out clearly even beneath the aged and loose flesh of his cheeks and neck. In asking its question, the voice had taken on a malevolent tone. "But not one tenth so bad as I will get you," it said.

"Fie on you, demon!" Rev. Fort ejaculated. "What has John Bell done to deserve your retribution?"

The spirit said no more that evening. What was very clear by what it had already revealed, however, was that it had an intimate knowledge of what went on in the neighbourhood, even from years before it made itself known. In my log, I noted that this might mean it was somehow a person or persons who had long lived in Red River. I know that magicians have existed since the time of Moses, as were the priests of Pharaoh, and that many apparently impossible feats have been accomplished by these talented tricksters. How all the "witch's" manifestations could have been managed without detection, I did not know, but I was still more inclined to believe in a natural explanation than in a supernatural one.

My rational beliefs were scotched once and for all a few Mondays later, on April 26. The population of Red River was pretty fairly divided between Baptists and Methodists. I had been born and raised Presbyterian. I was used to being shepherded by a minister whose full time work it was to learn the subtleties of theology, to hone his homilies, and to attend to the needs of his flock. Of course, the Baptists did not believe in hiring a pastor and so relied on the fervent energies of self-supporting men who enjoyed preaching and teaching. On the frontier at that time, the Methodists either depended on paid circuit-riding ministers or else imitated the Baptists and licensed by vote shepherds from among their own. Consequently, every tenth man in Red River was called "Reverend."

Unfortunately, the denomination of my fathers was not as zealous in its missionary work as were the Baptists or Methodists. The Presbyterian church at that time turned its attention upon only places of some concentrated population and outward refinement such as Nashville, where men wore ruffled shirt fronts and beaver hats and women silk dresses and leghorn bonnets. I was content to commune with God under the various church rooves [sic] of the community, careful on account of my need for subscription pupils to favour no denomination over the other.[10]

On Sunday the 25th of April, I attended Bethel Methodist Church, which was led by Rev. Thomas Gunn. One of the day's readings was from the fourth chapter of Acts, in which the elders of the synagogue required of Peter and John by what power they had made a crippled man walk. Rev. Gunn based his sermon upon this passage, exhorting us not only to do good works amongst our neighbours and especially amongst those less blest than us but also to do the works in the name of Jesus Christ, reminding ourselves and those helped of the source of all strength. Among the hymns that Brother Gunn lined for us was one whose words were written by John Wesley, "Jesus, Thy Boundless Love to Me." Its four verses were a particular favourite of mine.

The next morning, I had just awakened when I heard a knocking at my door. John Bell stood outside in the cool morning, with a wild look in his eyes and his shirt misbuttoned. I invited him inside for tea.

"Did you attend services at either Drake's Pond or Bethel Methodist yesterday?" he asked.

I answered him.

"Can you remember in any detail the Bible passages read, the sermon, or the hymns?"

These, too, I supplied. The look on John's face remained mazed. I asked if this had something to do with the spirit that haunted his house.

"It does," he replied. "Last night, both Reverends Sugg Fort and Thomas Gunn paid visits upon me. We had the whole family in the house, as well as both Johnston families, and were discussing a passage from St. Mark when the damned witch chimed in. It said, 'That point could be elucidated by the sermon you preached today, Reverend Gunn. Tell everyone what you said.'

" 'How do you know what I preached?' Thomas says.

" 'Because I was there and heard it,' it says.

" 'You are lying again,' Thomas says.

" 'Am I?' it came back. And then her voice moved from near the hallway up to our altar, and with a sound something very close to Thomas's voice began to recite the Bible passages for the day, to line every hymn, preach his sermon word for word, and pronounce the closing prayer. While it droned on, Thomas several times affirmed that the performance was a perfect duplication. Once the spirit was done imitating the service, it proceeded to analyze the points of the sermon and to criticize it.

" 'You should be relieved that she did not attend your service, Brother Fort, for now you have the advantage,' James Johnston remarked.

" 'I can tell you what Old Sugg said as well,' it says.

" 'And how can you do that?' James asked.

" 'Because I was there and heard him also,' it told us. And, once again, it reproduced the Baptist service word for word, as it had the one at Bethel. What's more, its voice changed to the likeness of Sugg's, using phrases of his style. Some expressed delight at the display, Dick, but I tell you it has frightened me more even than its ability to lash out against flesh."

I could see that John told the truth. He had not yet reached his three score years and ten, but he seemed all but a husk that morning.

"Did Sugg attest to the correctness of his words as the thing spoke it?" I asked.

"He did."

"And did any of your family or the Johnstons hear him over at Drake's Pond?"

"No. Everyone else was to Red River Baptist yesterday." John cast his eyes down in abject sorrow. "Except myself."

"Take heart in one fact, John; it has revealed another aspect of itself to us," I told him, endeavouring to make the shocking experience somewhat positive. "Since both services took place at eleven o'clock, and since the churches are more than ten miles distant from each other,

61

the thing cannot be a malicious neighbour but must indeed be supernatural."

"I agree. Yet perhaps it did not travel at all but rather read those men's minds at my house," John said. "And, perhaps, their souls as well."

I wonder if every man, no matter how vile or secretive, must unburden his sins to someone at some time. Certainly, despite our closeness, John had never made any dark confessions to me. I suspected from his look and words that he was about to do so then, fearing that the unwelcomed spirit would speak for him if he did not. I asked him directly if that was a reason for his early morning visit, and he shook his head.

"My sins are known to God," John said. "That is enough. But know you, Dick, that nothing I have done merits the torment visited by this unholy creature."

I assured him that I did not think it could be otherwise. Moreover, even if he had somehow fooled every member of the Red River community by an outwardly righteous life, what reason would that have been for the entity to torture also his entire family and, in particular, to attack Betsy physically? He merely shook his head again, finished his tea, and bade me good morning.

In the most harrowing of times, be it war, famine or pestilence, the urge for man and woman to leave their parents and find mates can not be denied. So it was in Red River. During the years of the "witch's" tenure, virtually all the young women between the ages of thirteen and sixteen within a few miles of the Bell farm attached themselves to ardent beaux. Rebecca Porter elicited complete devotion from James A. Long. Theny Thorn was just as spoilt by David Alexander Gooch's attentions as she had been by her adoptive parents, the James Johnstons. Also inseparable were James Darden and Lucinda Carr, Sarah Battle Fort and Joseph Wimberley, and Tempte Webb and Miles Gunn. Finally, celebrated and envied as the handsomest and most clever couple in the Red River area were Elizabeth Bell and Joshua Gardner. Of these pairs, all were married before 1821. All, that is, except your mother and Joshua Gardner. This was not of their choice but rather a direct intercession of the spirit that haunted the Bell farm.

By the spring of 1819, Joshua and Betsy had been tender to each other for two years. This situation was not at all to my liking, as I had myself become smitten by your mother upon first sight and came to love her soon after speaking with her and learning that her fairness of face and form were coupled with a sweet disposition, a ready wit, and a facile mind. But I was, as I had said to her mother, considerably older than she and, what was more, her teacher. My nature opposed any thought of using my position of authority to gain an advantage over her affections. And so with a heavy heart I resigned myself to lose her to a younger suitor.

In order for me to be able to set aside money from my teaching, it was necessary to raise as much of my food as possible. One afternoon, after dismissing my pupils early, I went to work with my horse on two acres I had already plowed up for corn. I had already spaced the kernels in the furrows and was covering them over with a corn rock[11] when the spirit's feminine voice spoke my name as if walking beside me. I stopped short and whirled in a complete circle. There was no living thing except my horse within eyesight. In the clear afternoon light, I could see for hundreds of feet, to where the land rolled downward toward the river and upward toward the Brown's

Ford–Springfield Road. I felt as if I had been hit in the jaw with a flying plow handle.

"Betsy and Joshua will soon announce their engagement," it said, with no preamble. "You must act now, before it happens."

"And why should I do that?" I asked the thin air.

"Because you love Betsy Bell."

"That is none of your affair," I told it, and chucked the reins to start the horse forward again.

"Oh, is it not? I can make it my affair. And if you do nothing, I will certainly make this engagement my affair."

"Why are you so intent on denying Betsy happiness?" I asked.

"That is my affair," it said, laughing.

"You profess to know all, including the future," I said.

"Do I?"

"You certainly made a prediction concerning John Jr. and his chances with the young lady who has recently arrived in Port Royal from Virginia," I reminded it.

"True. And what of it, O Learned Teacher?"

"If I were to step in and press my suit, would I succeed with Betsy?"

"Most assuredly," it said. It sounded as if it were humming with pleasure.

"And what proof can you offer me?"

This silenced it for several seconds. "I offer you nothing, except the promise that I will not beat you into a simpleton if you do enter the lists."

"I have no fear of you," I told the thing, although I certainly had. "You offer nothing; I will do nothing."

I had hoped it would offer me a plausible path in my pursuit of Betsy, but it would not be baited. Rather than be used and turned into the object of a prank, as John

Bell had with the Indian's tooth, I elected to continue in my depressing state of immobility.

The creature was not to be thwarted. In June, part of the community gathered on the Bell front lawn for a pick-nick [sic]. I used that time to tend to my crops and elected not to attend, especially as I knew the announcement that was to be forthcoming. Present were the Johnston clan, the Gunn clan, some of the Forts, the Dardens, and John and Patience Whitehead Gardner and their son Joshua. The Gardners were especially welcome, as John operated a still out at Purnell's Branch and would bring a jug or two of "the demon" to celebrations. John was especially liberal this day, as his son had confided to him his intention to wed Betsy Bell.

At a certain lull in the pick-nick, Joshua stood up among the revelers and called for attention. Before he could say his piece, the familiar voice of the "Bell witch" interrupted.

"It is a noble desire Joshua Gardner has," it said, in a rather subdued tone. "He wishes to marry Betsy Bell and take her away from my presence. He thinks she can escape as her sister Esther did. But Esther and Betsy are different. What he does not understand is that I can follow Betsy anywhere. I can circle the wide world and be back here in a minute. I will follow her if you wed her, Josh, be it to Siam. Please don't marry him, Betsy Bell. Don't marry Joshua Gardner!"

Having ruined the moment, it disappeared. As a body, the gathering began voicing opinions on what the young couple should do. Betsy, whose face had become scarlet, raced into the house, with Joshua following after her. The debate did not let up, although the pick-nick had for all intents come to an end. In the following days, no one had the temerity to ask either Joshua or Betsy what they had decided. All realized that a concerted silence about the matter was the surest means to keep the witch from venting its fury upon your mother.

Between April and July, the spirit made numerous visits to the Bell home, most often just before bed time and always directly after Betsy was struck with a fit. It delighted in sharing the gossip of the day and, in fact, leading the pack of wagging tongues. It reported every person who had not been to church of a Sunday, who had slept during the sermons, every person who took too many horns of liquor, who had idled away hours, what woman was a nagging shrew, what man beat his children, et cetera. So ruthless was the thing in disclosing sins and foibles that Red River became a paragon among wilderness communities.

It also delighted in engaging in discussions on good and evil and quoting from the Bible. In between its lies and spewage of such words as "damned," "whore," "asshole," and many far worse that I choose not to set down, it perversely praised the leading of a Christian life. Christianity it declared to be the true religion. It steadfastly declared Jesus Christ to be King of Kings and the only true path to salvation.

By this time, the news of the invisible, speaking phenomenon at the Bell farm had spread far and wide. Every night the house was filled with those hoping to witness with their own eyes and ears this wonder of the world. The Bells had half a dozen straw mattresses made so that guests could be accommodated on the floors of the dining room and social room. Sometimes the number was so great that all could not be fit inside the house and so had to tent out on the front lawn. Most brought their own tents which they had sewn for camp meetings, but here again the Bells supplied shelter to any who had not come prepared. They also stabled the numerous horses and offered every visitor victuals. On every occasion John refused recompense, so scrupulous was he in preventing anyone from accusing his family of making a profit off their troubles. Most visitors were polite and respectful of property.

Others were of the meanest nature. A man named Jenkins who hailed from miles away but who had a reputation bad enough to be known even in Red River eventually came to call. He was not content to keep his mouth closed and merely gawk but stuck his oar in during a discussion that the "witch" was leading regarding coveting a neighbour's property. Jenkins chimed in by remarking that he did not consider it a sin if a man were starving for lack of gainful employ and stole a piece of dried beef from a neighbour's smoke house to stay alive.

"Were you starving when you ate that sheepskin?" the spirit asked him, quick as lightning.

Jenkins blinked as if he had been given one of the slaps the thing doled out to your mother. Until the spirit departed, he behaved as if he had been struck dumb. Many eyes stole his way, however, as a missing sheepskin had been a mystery in the community several years past. As silence under accusation by the law assumes assent, if he had been standing trial in a human court his failure to defend himself against the spirit's remark would have condemned him. As it was, he took the first opportunity to quit the house and never returned. We never did learn whether the man had taken the sheepskin, but if he hadn't he must have realized the creature was believed by so many people that it would have been folly to deny it.

Indeed, after enough demonstrations of its omniscience, too many were gulled into taking as gospel every word that issued from the thing's unseeable throat.

The "witch" might have gained limitless power over the community if it had been willing to tell only truths. But such control was clearly not its purpose in haunting the Bell house, for every now and then it told a lie that was designed to be found out.

The main question put to the disembodied voice was "Who or what are you?" Up until the end of June of 1819, it had never given any direct answer except that it was a disturbed spirit made unhappy. Frequently, it would appear to answer obliquely by quoting passages of scripture from the Bible. Other times, it would ask the interrogator what he or she thought and appear satisfied to have the question answered on its behalf. Finally, however, James Gunn cannily declared to the thing that it probably could not answer, as it had no idea what it was or how it had been made.

"I know exactly who I was," it replied, "and I have been waiting for you to ask, Jim. You are one of the only ones who ask intelligent questions, and so you deserve an honest reply. I was one of the first white men to explore this region."

"Were you killed here?" Gunn asked.

"No, but I was killed. Indians killed me."

"Why did you return here?"

"Because this place was among the most beautiful in my explorations, a place where I found peace. In fact, I had planned to return here before my life was cut short. The proof of this is that I buried nearby almost all the money I had."

James Gunn laughed. "Well, it is said that you can't take anything with you when you go."

"That is true enough. So, I want to give the money to Betsy Bell."

James Johnston, who was present at least every third night since his first invitation, was one of several close friends of the family there that evening. Before the crowd could discuss this remarkable offer, he spoke up.

"It is about time you gave the poor girl some recompense for all the suffering you have dealt her, especially seeing as you refuse to tell us why that is."

"Where is this money?" Mr. Gunn asked.

"I will say nothing until my conditions are met."

"State them!" said James Gunn. "We are all as family here tonight. Betsy Bell need have no fear that anyone will steal the money from her."

"First," the voice said, "every note and coin must go to Betsy alone."

"Agreed."

"Second, three persons and three persons only must dig the money from the earth. They are Drewry Bell, Bennett Porter, and Old Sugar Mouth."

After Betsy, Drewry was the individual most cuffed by the creature. He was, therefore, loath to involve himself in anything suggested by the "witch," but it refused to divulge the money's hiding place until he relented. Alexander Bennett Porter was your Aunt Esther's husband, and he loved laughing and joking with the thing. He was willing to hear the creature out. James had a mighty antipathy toward it but no outward fear. The thing's choices seemed as curious as they were diverse.

Once all three men agreed to the creature's particulars,

it disclosed that the money was in a box under a large flat rock that lay just beside a spring in the southwest corner of the Bell property. The spring emptied into the Red River as the river completed a large horseshoe turn. It was a well-known place. I myself used the spring's waters and had trod upon that prodigious rock many times.

The three men set out at dawn the next morning. I was made aware of the spirit's revelation early in the day and about noon walked down to see how much progress had been made. The participants had brought a mattock and shovel for digging, as well as an axe whereby they cut and fashioned from large saplings several stout prizes. As I approached, they had already spent some five hours on the project and had only just managed to swivel the stone away.

I told the three that I hoped their work was not in vain. It seemed to me first of all unlikely that one of the first woodsmen out in the wilderness would have had a reason to be carrying a great sum of cash. Rather, he should have carried barter, to trade with the Indians. Secondly, if three strong men with good tools needed five hours to move this rock, how could an explorer with likely no more than flintlock, knife, and axe be able to move it? I concluded by saying that since the creature that had put them up to this folly could tear the bed clothes out of the hands of the likes of Frank Miles, I would have invited it to do the hard work itself.

The three agreed with me on all counts but declared that they had come too far now to quit. They were further heartened by the observation that they had found leaves and sticks in the dirt beneath the stone, suggesting that it had indeed been moved in recent times. When I quit them, they had decided that the box might be buried at some depth beneath the rock.

That evening, I walked over to the Bell farm. Bennett had gone home, but Drewry and James were there. They explained to the family how they had scraped and dug with mattock and hands until a hole had been made, about six feet on each side and almost as deep. No box had been found. Directly after Betsy recovered from her evening fit, the "witch" appeared, cackling with great mirth over the joke it had played. As if it had been standing all day right where I had briefly stood, it related the futile enterprise to the gathering, quoting each man's remarks, including mine. Particularly scornful was it of the way in which "Old Sugar Mouth" had stood in the shade of a nearby tree and encouraged the younger men from a distance.

James Gunn had come back to the farm specifically to see what had happened. He was not one of the several who laughed along with the spirit.

"You told me last night that I deserved an honest reply from you," he reminded, tossing cold water upon the general glee. "You lied."

"But at least I did not make you pay for my lie, like Old Sugar Mouth did," it said. Some laughed. Mr. Gunn, John Bell, and I did not.

Soon after this, it told John Johnston that it was a "witch" conjured up by his own stepmother. A few days later it told Calvin Johnston, John's nephew, that it was the spirit of a three-year-old boy who had died in North Carolina and been left behind when his family moved to Red River. Careful checking revealed no such child had ever existed. Eventually, the thing recanted both lies and laughed loudly at the fact of its own prevarication.

71

The other lie it told at this time it never admitted to be such. This provided the final nails for Kate Batts's coffin as far as most of the community were concerned.

Rev. James Gunn was much more vexed and frustrated by the spirit than his brother, Thomas. He never relented in posing his question: "Who are you, and what do you want?"

On July 11, the spirit answered him. "You are a good man, Brother Gunn, and therefore I won't lie to you; I am Kate Batts's witch."

This elicited many gasps from around the crowded room, but Jim shook his head and said, "When you spoke about the money buried under the rock, you told me that was an honest reply. Why should I believe you now?"

"Because I am tired of lying, and you deserve the truth more than any other man in this room. I am Old Kate Batts's witch for certain. It was she, dancing around a pentagram, who conjured me here."

"For what purpose?"

"Why, to torment her enemy, John Bell. To torment him to his death."

Rev. Gunn raised his hands to silence the troubled throng. "You have had much sport at our expense," he said to the spirit. "If you wish me to believe you now, you must atone with some proof of what you say."

"How much proof do you need?" it answered. "Old Kate has already hounded John in court. She will not mount her horse because she is a weirding one. You know that she roams the land looking to borrow pins. She has left them all in a stump in the woods, so that I may stick them in John Bell. And that is what I will soon do. Then you will have your proof. Old Kate wants John dead, and I will see to it for her."

It seemed no use for James, myself, or even John Bell to argue with most of the community that the spirit was once again dealing in a lie. Too many were set to fix the Bell family suffering upon Kate Batts's human agency.

As if the spirit's condemnation was not enough, the local goodies began assembling their own tales to help prove Kate Batts the culprit. One was a Fort wife who lived just across the Red River from the Batts farm. She was quite effective and zealous about spreading the word of an incident she declared had happened to her. On a churning day, she was having no luck after much time turning the milk into butter. Slapping the dasher with angry energy, she declared, "I do believe Old Kate Batts has put a hex upon my churn. Well, I'll burn the hell out of this milk." With that, she snatched a poker from the fireplace and plunged it into the milk. According to her, after that the milk practically turned to butter without churning. Not content at her sudden change of luck, she decided to cross the river and look in on Kate. The poor woman had evidently just burned her hand by grabbing a poker too close to the hot end.

I am convinced, especially because I had some slight acquaintance with this loose-tongued Fort wife, that this story was created backwards. Whatever the truth, the sight of Kate Batts parading through the neighbourhood with her hand wrapped in a bandage was enough to turn many fence sitters against her for ever. Worse, however, was that this ready solution to the great mystery caused too many souls to stop inquiring as to the real origin and purpose of what they were all happily calling "Kate's witch." How wide they were off the mark they never learned. I, who have been too generously praised through the years for my learning and keen mind, whilst never

73

believing that the thing was Kate Batts's doing, nevertheless was a blind man though sighted and a deaf man with hearing, until forced to see and hear more than a decade later.

In the middle of August, 1819, the community, myself included, was invited to the wedding of Miss Tembte Webb to Mr. Miles Gunn. It was a splendid outdoor affair, doubly splendid owing to Old Kate's consideration in not making her presence known. Nevertheless she was there, as evidenced by several remarks she later passed which proved the case.

The wedding and its preparation were so diverting that, for a time, even those of us within sight of the Bell farm were not thinking of the "witch" very often. I believe it may have been out of jealousy for its faded fame that the spirit contrived to offer us a new wonder. This was the creation of a number of personalities. According to Old Kate, she was really a family of spirits that had come to plague the Bell family. This was how, she averred, she was able to hear two sermons being preached at the same hour although miles distant from each other. I, however, never saw enough difference in the pack of personalities to think that they were more than roles put on by the same spirit, as the famous David Garrick might variously take on Richard III, Othello, Hamlet, or Hotspur. What is more, I believe they were inspired by a sermon Rev. Gunn had not long before given. The good pastor had been obsessed since the spirit's appearance with passages of demoniac possession in the Bible, and on this occasion he preached about the man from Gerasenes who was possessed of an unclean spirit and who told Jesus his name was Legion, "because we are many."

Even though the spirit continued to answer happily to

"Old Kate," she offered up four characters with the singular names of Black Dog, Cypocryphy, Jerusalem, and Mathematics. Black Dog, it was clear, was inspired by John Bell's frequently related account of his first supposedly supernatural encounter. This character took charge and often bossed the other voices about. Both its tone and its language were harsh, although the underlying sound was nonetheless female. Cypocryphy took credit for the jokes and gossip gathering and spoke in a high, very feminine tone. Jerusalem sounded like a boy before his voice changes, and he was the one who most often protested that he spoke the truth. In fact, the spirit used this voice whenever it especially wanted to be believed, and I can not recall a time when it initiated a statement that was untrue. Mathematics also had a feminine voice and came out when logic and religion were being discussed. However, whenever the spirit appeared at an event that involved drinking of liquor, Mathematics could always be counted upon to become magically inebriated and to argue with the coarse Black Dog in a like manner, uttering the most barbarous phrases.

Sometimes, all four voices would alternate with each other in what appeared to be drunken brawls. Often, combined with the shouting, could be heard the noises of pots and pans clattering and dogs barking. As with its other exhibitions, once this quadriga appeared, it never departed for longer than a week or two.

In the beginning of September, when the summer term of school had ended, I took myself one morning down to the Red River to do some fishing. I remember this incident most clearly, even without need of my log. It was a Monday, which was always washing day, early enough that nothing had yet gone up on lines. Lucy Bell was standing on the river bank supervising the darkie girls at the kettle and the scrub boards. When she saw me, she gave them a few commands and then asked if I would accompany her a little ways upstream.

Your grandmother engaged me in light discourse for a time, whilst above us songbirds warbled and to our left the river burbled. I recall her remarking with pleasure that I wore the moccasins she had made me for my birthday. I could see immediately, however, that something was troubling her mind. Soon enough, she told me that she had had a private talk with Betsy the previous evening, when they were repairing quilts that the spirit had mutilated.

Out of a blue sky, Betsy said to her mother, "You speak to the witch very seldom."

"That is true," Lucy answered.

"It seems to like you, mother."

"That is also true, although I do not encourage its affection."

"Could you not take advantage of its tender feelings towards you and ask it why it torments me so fiercely?"

"I have, Betsy. Whenever it seems particularly humoured by my conversation and we are alone, I always ask it of its nature and purpose. Especially its purpose in attacking you and in speaking out against your father. It straight out refuses to answer. It is most apologetic about its refusal, but it will not be moved."

They went on sewing in silence together for a time, and then Betsy spoke again.

"Mother, I have heard the preachers read from the Bible that some men and women have committed such terrible sins that their families are punished for generations afterwards. Do you know of any one in either your family history or father's that was so terrible?"

Lucy's heart was dashed by her daughter's pathetic words. She answered that she truthfully knew of no blemish on either family, no justification for such a supernatural visitation. After that, Betsy sank into silence until the sewing was done.

Having told me of this, Lucy stopped walking and faced me.

"I have been thinking that this may soon drive her mad," she said, speaking of your mother. "I know that the witch says it can follow any one to the ends of the earth, but it has also lied many times. These nightly spells are driving Betsy to despair. Do you think it is worth the risk to remove her from this place?"

"Are you thinking to send her back to your relatives in North Carolina?" I asked.

"No. That would be too simple for the witch to reason out. I was thinking that you could take her away. Hear me out, Dick. You are learned and capable of making a living anywhere. Perhaps this thing could not exist in a city, even if it found you two there. We could have Rev. Fort or Rev. Gunn marry you secretly, and then you could take Betsy away without telling any one of your destination. Not even me."

"And if the creature made good its boast and did find us?" I replied. "What then?"

"You could always return here. At least it has not spoken out against you, as it has with Josh Gardner."

I sat down on a rock to ponder Lucy's words. My heart leapt, both from the idea of marrying the young woman I so adored and at the prospect of being able to save her. But I was also troubled.

"If Betsy were indeed found at a distance by this creature, she would not there have the love and support of her family," I answered. "All the burden of keeping up her pluck would fall upon me. And I am not even sure that she would be happy to be wed to me. That alone might distress her. Marriage in itself is a trial, Mrs. Bell. Marriage under such circumstances would be fair neither to Betsy nor to me."

"Yes. I understand," Lucy said, surprising me at her lack of conviction in her idea.

I stood and helped your grandmother up. "I have a counter proposal. If Betsy's fits become worse or if she begins to act as if she is truly losing her mind, I will marry her and take her away. There is only one other requirement: she must be content with the idea of marriage to me. I do not demand that my love for her be requited, but she must at least feel at ease with the union."

At my words, Lucy looked much relieved. She held out her hand for shaking. "Agreed."

We walked downriver together, remarking on the coming fall, both doing our best to avoid reopening the delicate subject. I was glad that I had planned to devote that morning only to fishing, as I had trouble mustering enough concentration even to keeping my eye on three poles.

As soon as the spirit identified itself as "Old Kate Batts's witch," many in the community forgot about its other lies in this regard and grew satisfied that they now knew both its origin and purpose. The rest of us went right on trying to reason out the mystery. The keystone question seemed to be why the manifestation also fixed its fury on Betsy Bell.

One who refused to stop badgering the spirit for answers was John Johnston. John often declared that if he were rich he would have spent his free time becoming a scientist. His frequent visits to the Bell farm were for two stated purposes: the first was to divert the spirit from its exhausting assaults upon the Bells. The second was to plumb the depths of the spirit's secrets. Towards both ends, he used his garrulous nature to good effect. Old Kate seemed very entertained by Mr. Johnston's patter, his jokes, gossip, ruminations on certain passages of the Bible, et cetera. She also seemed flattered by his many practical petitions of her wisdom regarding impending weather, the whys and hows of planting, the questions of the operations of the wider world.

One evening, Mr. Johnston chanced to have the spirit all to himself in the social room, and he hopped on the opportunity.

"I want to thank you, Kate, for being so kind to me and teaching me so many things."

"That is all right, John," it replied. "You are kind to me and deserve the same in return."

"I am gratified. But there is one thing you have not told me nor anyone else: what is your nature?"

"Ah. That I cannot tell you. Not yet, leastways."

"When, then?"

"When I am ready to leave this place."

"And when will that be?"

"I cannot tell you that precisely either. All you can know is that I will not leave until Old Jack Bell dies."

Mr. Johnston nodded. A joke came to him, to lull the spirit into believing that he did not consider this a serious discussion.

"Surely you do not mean that you will kill him?"

"I mean exactly that."

For all the wicked acts and obscene words that the creature had directed at John Bell, it had not before that moment stated plainly that this was its plan. John Johnston jumped in his seat.

"But what reason could you have for such a terrible deed?" he asked it.

"My own reason."

"Has he committed a sin so horrible that he should deserve murder?"

"Let us just say that I dislike him enough to kill him."

Now, Mr. Johnston felt it incumbent upon himself to turn the powerful being from its fell intent.

"Do you not know, Kate, that John Bell is one of the most respected, well-liked men in all of this land?"

There was a silence for a moment. Then, in a soft voice, it said, "I do. And that is why he needs killing."

John told me later that he had all he could do not to run from the room. Instead, he counseled himself to a stouter degree of mental grit and determined that, since the spirit was talking and, moreover, talking with a tone of voice that he had come to know meant it was serious, then he must stay with it and draw forth every bit of its intent. He cast about for a sly method to uncover the creature's motivation despite its reluctance to disclose it.

"But if you do kill Old Jack and give us no better reason than that," John argued, "then we will all think it very hard of you, and the law will see that you are hanged for murder without cause."

The spirit laughed. "If Frank Miles could not catch me with all his strength, how do you propose to hold me long enough to hang me? You know the saying, John: 'It's catchin' before hangin.'"

"And do you propose to kill Betsy Bell as well?"

"No. Why do you think I would kill Betsy?"

"Because you torture her and follow her wherever she goes, shout at her, slap her, and pull her hair. You have forbidden her to marry. I certainly think that proves you hate her."

"Perhaps I am jealous, as a suitor would be. Don't lovers often bat each other about playfully?"

"I have never known any man who loves a woman to act as such," said John.

"How do you know that I am a man?"

"Well, you're certainly not a woman, the way you curse, and hit, and act like you're drunk. Are you a man?"

"I am a spirit. I live in the wind and in the water, inside houses and out, in Heaven and Hell. I am all things and nothing. Search your mind, John Johnston. Don't you know who I am?"

John did not, and he told the thing so. Shortly after, it departed from the room. John straightways found John and Lucy Bell and repeated the conversation several times. I got it the next day and set it down as you read it now.

The day after John Bell heard this report from Mr. Johnston, he was struck with another attack such as the one he had experienced visiting James Byrns for advice about the trial. As he described it, it was two feelings that united to form one torment. The first was like a double-pointed stick having been shoved crosswise into his mouth so that it poked against both jaws. The second was like a fungus growth upon the top and sides of his tongue, swelling it so much that he could not eat or speak during the hours of its appearance, nor hardly draw any air but through his nose.

81

John disclosed that he had experienced mild bouts of this affliction ever since the first occurrence but never so strong that he could not speak or eat. The business with the "witch" had been so dire that he simply bore the discomfort and told no one.

The spirit's death sentence on John Bell had another immediate and miraculous effect. From that moment on, Betsy's fits grew milder and milder until, within a month, they had disappeared, never to return. Her fits lessened in direct proportion to the increase of your grandfather's facial afflictions. As if the feeling of the sharp stick and the swelling fungus was not enough, over a period of months from September 1819 to January 1820, he also developed a twitching and rippling of the muscles that underlay his cheeks, jaw, and neck. The duration of his attacks also lengthened, right up to his death, such that they eventually might last for every one of his waking hours. Sometimes he would be entirely free of this for a day or two but never longer than that. This was the beginning of the curse that would rob him of all his vitality.[12]

Once the spirit had declared its purpose to John Johnston, and perhaps seeing how adversely the news had affected Old Jack, it began telling everyone in the community that it would not leave until it had seen that the patriarch of the Bell family had been done in. No one, however, could learn when this would happen or how. The spirit continued its mischievous pranks and its banter, as if it had announced John the winner of some lottery.

When Frank Miles was told how the "witch" had mentioned his inability to capture it, he went to John Bell and made an impassioned plea for the man to flee Red

River and save himself. The next night, when Old Kate paid her visit to the Bell farm, Frank was again on hand.

"So, here is Frank Miles, the Solomon of Red River," said the female voice. "You needn't have wasted your breath advising Old Jack to run away. Have I not said that I can follow any one to the ends of the earth?"

Having said her piece to him, she struck Frank such a blow that it knocked him over a high-backed chair.

"If you think you can avoid me, then you better had," it warned, "for I mean to give you a lot worse on the morrow. Try your best to hide from me, and together we will prove to Old Jack whether or not a person can escape."

Frank hightailed it next morning into Kentucky without telling anyone where he was headed, but true to the spirit's word she found and soundly thrashed him at a distance of twenty miles from the Bell farm. This event was kept as hushed as possible among the inner group of friends, but it convinced John that, whatever might come, he had to face it on his property. The spirit's demonstration also dashed forever my wild hope of running away with Betsy.[13]

When it became clear that John's affliction of the mouth was not going away by itself, Dr. George Hopson was brought to the farm. Dr. Hopson was in my opinion not deeply skilled or experienced as a physician. For one thing, he had many diversions from his doctoring, including the operation of a ferry service across the Red River. He was, though, the only doctor for many miles.[14]

Dr. Hopson's opinion upon examining your grandfather Bell was that it was a logical outcome of the "witch's" plaguing. John's entire nervous system was "aflame," he declared, and the physical manifestation of this had settled in his face. He prescribed avoidance of the creature as much as possible (I privately wondered if Hopson meant liquor, which many dubbed "the creature," as the doctor had never witnessed Old Kate's appearance and, along with most of the citizens of Port Royal, thought it nothing more harmful than a local joke), hot mustard plasters, and several tonics that had been known to have various successes at soothing the nerves. These remedies provided some little relief, but, despite Dr. Hopson's learned succour, John's mouth continued to dam up and his face to convulse.

Chloe was the old Negro woman on the Bell farm. She had been part of Lucy Williams's dowry. She had seven or perhaps eight children. Among these were her sons Dean and Harry, who were high-spirited and difficult for your grandfather Bell to keep under control, as well as Phyllis, Sally, Trisha, Anky, and Rachel, all good and obedient girls. If there was a sixth daughter, I can no longer remember her name or face. There were also two black men not related to Chloe, called Hack and Willis. The Bells' little tribe were of good heart and Christians, after their own peculiar fashion.[15] But they also were given to telling lies with all the wide-eyed ingenuousness of children. This, I think, was to compel attention of their owners, who it is true volunteered them little unless they were sick or idling. They also held on to old African beliefs, and these became mixed into both their behaviour and their story telling.

Some time after the darkies learned of the "witch," Rev. Gunn's patriarch slave Uncle Zeke began fashioning for the slaves what he called witch balls. They were intended to be wore around the neck or carried in a pocket, to ward off supernatural creatures. When I inquired of the contents of the vile-smelling object, I was told it contained animal excrement found in the woods, human semen, spit, sulphur, foxfire, and camphor, and was all wrapped up in woman's hair. How the Negroes could stand to wear these I will never know, because they were certain at least to ward off any natural creatures.

John Bell's right-hand man was a Negro of about thirty-five years' age named Dean. He was not very tall, but he was marvelously strong. No one in the county could fell a tree as quickly as Dean could, nor split a rail more truly. He also told the most fantastic tales. The following is an example of how people, black or white, invented personal encounters with the spirit, to call attention to themselves or to use it to excuse them of some action or inaction.

Dean had fathered a few children through a girl named Kate, who was the daughter of Uncle Zeke. After work hours, when the sun was just setting, Dean would walk the short distance between farms to be with her. She had learned from Zeke how to fashion witch balls and had lavished much time and care in making one to keep Dean safe. Not two days after receiving it, however, Dean had either lost it or else decided he could no longer abide the stench. When Kate took him to task for this, he said that he had kept silence so as not to frighten her but now she had forced him to speak of an encounter he had had with the witch.

Soon after John Bell told his story of meeting the big black dog, Dean had echoed that he, too, had met the witch in this disguise. Now he told his woman that he had had another such encounter with the dog, and that it had upbraided him for carrying the witch ball. Unless Dean tossed it out of his pocket, the spirit threatened to turn him into a horse and ride him across the Red River. According to Dean, when he produced the witch ball, it began to swell until he could no longer hold it. Then the huge ball burst into a stinking flame on the ground. Not content to leave the lie at that, Dean attested that the black beast began to growl and coiled back to leap upon him, wherewith he brought the axe he conveniently happened to be carrying down on its head, cleaving it into two parts. With that, the dog turned tail and disappeared. A few days later, Dean capped the tale by declaring that he had seen the same giant black dog at a distance, and that this time it had two whole heads.

Such stories were not the sole province of blacks. If you should wish to confirm among the long-time residents of Red River what I have here set down, be prepared to listen to more tall tales than truths.

Perhaps it was because of all the tall tales that Dean and the other darkies invented about the spirit that it loathed them so publickly. This it did not say, but it often complained about their smell, which odour is no wonder, since they work twice as hard as their masters and have the opportunity to bathe only half as often. Old Kate generally retreated from a room if a Negro servant was there, muttering words to the effect of "I can't stand the smell of a nigger; they stink up wherever they walk." Never to my knowledge did the spirit visit any of the slave quarters, which were within sight of the Bell farm house.

Lucy Bell was never discourteous to the spirit and often deigned to speak with it, in the hopes of getting it to reveal its true nature and mission. In her own private way, however, she despised the creature and, as is only natural in one's own home, tired of its frequent unwelcomed visits.

In the late fall of 1819, Lucy contrived a plan to keep the spirit out of her bedroom. This plan she shared with no one, her husband included, so as not to give the spirit any warning through overhearing an errant word. Chloe's daughter Anky was a full-grown girl and worked hard in the fields, thus emitting a pungent odor of sweat. Lucy approached her one day and said that she wanted to consider Anky for house duty. One of these duties would be to sleep inside the farm house. This was frightening to Anky, but Lucy reminded her that the witch had never bothered any of the Negroes whilst they slept. Thus was the girl convinced.

On the trial night, Anky brought her straw mattress into the Bells' bedroom and pushed it under Lucy's bed, which was one of the pieces fashioned in Baltimore which we had carried back from Nashville. Its four posts were elegantly turned, and its mattress lay quite high above the floor. Once under the bed, Anky and her mattress could not be seen because of the dust ruffles. As was the custom, Anky went directly to bed after her meal.

About an hour later, John, Lucy, and several of the children were seated in the parlour with several guests, being either persecuted or regaled by the female voice of Cypocryphy, depending upon the individual hearer's point of view. Of a sudden, the spirit's voice changed to the harsh tones of Black Dog.

"What is that smell?" it asked. It made several loud sniffing noises. "Has some one made an accident in their pants? No. It's nigger. Not the smell of Chloe or Phyllis that lingers from the afternoon and I am always forced to tolerate. It's coming from your bedroom, Luce."

The voice moved out of the sitting room and past the Bells' bedroom door.

"Here it is! It's that damned darkie Anky! She's under your bed."

As the group followed into the room, they heard the sounds of spitting from under the bed and then Anky's pitiful cries.

"Lawdy, Miss Lucy, it's spittin' me to death! I got to get out!"

Anky was a big girl and removed herself from under the bed with not a little trouble. Her actions, moreover, seemed to be slowed by the fact that she kept her hands over her face. She later testified that her cheeks, nose, and mouth were covered with white spittle, but no one in the group that witnessed her flight could vouch the same on account of her protecting hands. Once she was to her feet, she moved with remarkable alacrity. She could be heard screaming out of the house and all the way to the slave cabins.

"What's this mattress doing under the bed?" Black Dog asked. "Did you invite Anky to stay under here, Luce?"

"I did," Lucy answered, and then offered the spirit a taste of her own abilities to lie. "Anky showed a curiosity in hearing you sing and quote scripture. I know how much you dislike our Negroes, so I invited her to hide herself under my bed and listen through the open door."

"It's not just your niggers I hate," the voice declared. "It's all of their stinking race. Well, I guess she got more than she was expecting. If anybody but you had played this trick on me, I'd have killed the nigger. But this trick has turned back on you, Luce, because you'll be smelling nigger in your sleep for a month."

Despite proving the spirit's aversion to Negroes, owing to its vile oath and the darkies' redoubled terror after the incident, Lucy elected never to repeat the experiment. She did, however, find the "witch" true to its word and was able to hide from it in her bedroom for an entire month.

Another curiosity of the spirit came to light in the late fall of 1819. Undoubtedly, the family most involved with the "witch" after the Bells themselves were the Johnston clan. James, the father, shied away from the Bell estate as soon as he learned of the troubles. His sons, John and Daniel Calvin (known only as Calvin), however, seemed to take a positive joy in the spirit's presence, even as they commiserated with the Bells. They perpetually anticipated the appearance of a newspaper person from Baltimore, Philadelphia, or New York who would note their closeness to the "witch" and make them famous throughout the broad land. I am glad to say this never happened, but the Johnston men nevertheless seemed to court the spirit's favours. Each used his own particular personality to appeal to Old Kate. Calvin took an earnest, honest approach in his intercourse. John was more devious and full of guile. Thus, John was ever engaged in persiflage, hoping to lull the spirit off its guard. In this, he was continuously confounded.

One evening when I was not present, the discussion came about with Old Kate how it could be incorporeal to the extent that it did not even cast a shadow under sun or fire light but yet it could deliver stinging blows. While neither Calvin nor John had been the recipients of such attacks, they had heard the unmistakable sound of flesh meeting flesh and seen the pink or red imprints of something like a hand upon the cheeks of Betsy and Drewry.

"I am the mystery of mysteries," Old Kate answered.

"That I will grant," said Calvin. "But if you can give a

smack, then surely you can deliver a simple and cordial hand shake."

"To who?" the spirit asked.

Calvin reported that he shrugged. "Oh, let us say to me."

"Why should I?"

"Because we are friends."

"Are we?"

"Shame on you!" John swam in. "You have cut my brother to the quick. Only last week you told half a dozen strangers that he was the most polite man in Red River and one of the only people you trusted."

"A few kind words on my part do not necessarily make him my friend."

"Then let us shake on our friendship," Calvin said, "and prove to the world that you are not universally despised."

A long silence was reported, wherein those present supposed the challenge had frightened the spirit away. But a minute later, the voice of Mathematics sang out loudly.

"I will shake your hand, Calvin Johnston, on one condition."

"And what is that?"

"That you promise to neither close your fingers around nor grab me when I touch you."

"Agreed."

Calvin is an honest man; he is also clever. He angled himself close to the fire so that any disturbance of the air might be glimpsed by the others around him. He wiped his hand against his trousers and then held it out. Those who watched testified that his hand lowered an inch or two, as if pressing downwards. Calvin himself reported that the sensation was not at all unpleasant, feeling light and smooth, like the hand of a petite lady. If anyone in the community could be believed, it was Daniel Calvin Johnston. This incident went a long way towards verifying that the spirit was indeed an independent entity and not some trick of sounds and threads caused by the Bell family. No one saw any movement in the air or shadow against the fire, however.

"Am I not as good a friend to you?" John Johnston addressed the empty space in front of Calvin, at the same time holding out his hand.

The "witch" laughed. "No, you are not, John. I know your game. You are nice for treacherous reasons. If I gave you my hand, you would try to catch me."

"I will lay the same hand first on the Bell Bible and swear to behave just as good as Cal," John protested.

"You could swear by the loss of your private parts and I would not trust you, Johnny," Black Dog said. "You're a scoundrel and a rascal, and I trust you not at all. If you want a sample of my fist upon your face, however, I will be glad to oblige you."

Ever after, John complained to Old Kate about the unfairness of favouring his brother with her hand, but he protested for naught.

It was Tuesday, October 12, that John Jr. returned home from North Carolina empty handed, as I have already written. On Sunday, the 10th, the spirit reported that John was safe and less than a hundred miles from the farm. Likewise, on the 11th, it predicted that he would arrive on the next day or the day after. When he arrived, late in the evening, a number of neighbours entered the farm with him, so firmly had they trusted the spirit's predictions and been on the look-out. He was asked by more than one if he had noticed any ghostly figures or large animals in his recent path. Rather peevishly, he replied that he had not. He also reminded every one that he had posted a letter a month previous that had managed to be delivered, declaring that he expected to be home by the middle of October. Given this advance notice, he did not count the "witch's" prediction so miraculous.

The spirit seemed to have great respect for John Jr. I believe his lack of awe over its prediction of his return inspired it to give a similar but more miraculous example of its abilities. As the days of 1819 grew shorter and the nights longer, the cold began to set in. A trip away from home in November or December was viewed with some degree of alarm, as snow or ice might blow in at any time and isolate the traveler miles from any shelter.

Thus it was that Jesse was occasioned to be up in Kentucky purchasing several horses, with his schedule for returning home entirely dependent upon how long it took to locate and acquire the breed he required. When Jesse married Martha Gunn, he was given at a low price lands from both the Gunn and Bell estates. This put his new hearth about a mile from the Bell farm house. It was far enough away that Lucy could not peek over between stirs of the kettle.

The night of the day that Jesse had predicted he might be back, Lucy inquired at the supper table if any one had seen him. No one had. With that, the spirit, which had been silent throughout the meal, spoke up.

"Wait just a minute, Old Luce. I shall go and see for you."

True to its word, it was back inside the minute, bringing news that Jesse not only was home but sitting at a certain table, reading by the light of a candle. When Jesse came to visit his mother the next morning, he said that he had arrived home chilled in the near darkness and had not wanted to venture out again until daybreak. When asked if he had taken up a book the previous night, he confirmed that he had and, what was more, had read at a table by candle rather than fire light. Most amazingly, he reported that while he read there had been a knock on his front door. Before he could rise to answer it, the latch had flown up, it had opened on its own and then immediately closed again.

"I guessed that it was the witch checking up on me," Jesse told his mother.

Just before Jesse left on his buying trip, Drewry had announced that he had started building a flatboat down on the Red River, had it cabled to a stout tree, and that he and young Sandy Johnston wanted to float it down to New Orleans, just as he, John Jr., and Alexander Porter had done a few years before.[16]

"It's not a good idea, with Jesse going away," John Bell had told him at the supper table.

"But we have had such a good year in both tobacco and pigs," Drewry pleaded. "We could get holiday prices for everything."

"Not if you're dead," the spirit broke in. "Two is not enough to navigate and keep a rifle trained on the sawyers.[17] The river pirates are still thick at Friar's and Montgomery's Points."

On the previous trip, John Jr. had acted as look out. He had become a dead eye at shooting, as he had served under Andrew Jackson in the second war against the British. As you know, he is also a very big and strong man and would present a daunting figure atop a flatboat. Without him, the venture would be very risky.

Much as he wanted to agree with the spirit for once,

John Sr. declined to comment. It was up to Lucy to echo the spirit's concerns and declare the notion of such a trip dead.

Old Kate undoubtedly saved more in both body and soul through her words. There were, as I have written, many who had come west to find their promised land but who also did not believe it was a gift from God. These men and women chose not to spend their time or money repaying the Almighty by becoming members of any church denomination. It was also common that these were the men who most often got drunk and who beat their wives and children, and women who were less than good and attentive mothers. That they chose not to join the local churches was their business, but they could not survive long without the aid and support of the other members of the community. Old Kate reported these folks' failings with regularity, and the subsequent cold treatment by the community, not to say the sharp gossip, usually resulted in some bettering of their bad habits.

Life moved apace into 1820, with the spirit coming and going with regularity at the Bell farm and elsewhere about the Red River area. For a long while it took on no new habits, names, or voices. Rarely did it make its presence known beyond engaging in nighttime discussions. Its perorations about points of theology became less and less dialogues with the guests and more and more monologues. Around the New Year of 1820, its favourite theme was the weighing of justification by faith against justification by good works. According to the spirit, if one had true faith in Jesus as saviour, then good works must follow as proof of that faith. Professed belief alone was worth nothing. Such faith was not true. Moreover, it did not admit that Jesus was the only way to God, but that some one who did good works sincerely and without an eye on earning eternal salvation could merit it nonetheless.

Added to all this religion, the spirit's singing voice became sweeter and sweeter. Chary as she was to engage in intercourse with the thing, Lucy seemed unable to keep from praising its music, and often went so far as to request certain hymns. Devoted as it was to your grandmother's happiness, it always obliged.

It sleeted and rained a fair part of March and April in 1820, so much so that all of us longed mightily to get outside of our dark walls. For some months, the entire community had become dependent upon the "witch's" weather predictions, which were twice as accurate as any almanack [sic]. In the fall of 1819, they had petitioned it to tell them dry spells for harvesting and how long before a killing frost would set in. That spring, they were setting their planting schedules by its words. As it had predicted, the rain never seemed to halt for long. It seemed that every other day, Old Kate was forecasting a nasty downpour or a stiff gale.

Finally, in May the skies cleared. Your mother, Richard Williams, and Becky Porter decided to take advantage of the weather and go for a ride. As they were saddling their horses, the spirit came into the barn and told them that they had better not go. A violent storm was breezing up from the north, she said. As she had been reporting such things for many months and some of the weather turned out much milder than she made it out to be, the three young people chose to ignore her.

They rode northwest, to take the first ford in the river and head toward Keysburg. When they reached the river, however, they realized that it was still quite swollen. They paused to debate their choices, and where their horses stood was a thick stand of mature poplar trees. One, in fact, still held the cable of what was left of Drewry's flatboat.

As the three debated, a wind storm did sweep in suddenly from the north. The trees began swaying, and leaves that had only sprung from their branches weeks before were stripped off and blown high into the sky. Richard voiced his opinion that these giant trees offered the best shelter and that if they tried to ride home, they would be blown off their mounts.

"You're wrong, boy!" one of the spirit's voices cried out over the moaning of the wind. "If you stay here you'll be crushed. These poplars will not bend as willows do. Get to the other side of the river now!"

"But it's too high. We could drown," Becky feared aloud.

"You won't. Go!"

Despite the spirit's direction, the three decided to head for the Bell farm. The horses, however, would not be guided. They reared up or shied sideways.

The spirit called out again.

"You little fools! Hold tight to the reins but do or say nothing to the horses!"

Without direction from the young people, the horses turned as one and moved with speed down the bank, plunging fearlessly through the roiling river. Nor did they stop until they had reached a sheltering stand of boulders, where Betsy, Becky, and Richard were able to dismount and wait the storm out. When they returned by the same route on which the spirit had led them, they found several of the trees in their path uprooted, with mighty branches scattered about. There was no doubt in your mother's mind that one or more of them would have been killed had it not been for Old Kate's intervention. I myself surveyed the scene once the storm had passed, and I agreed.

The next month, a party of young people decided to explore the cave that the Bells used for storing food. As you have never been there, I should describe it. The bluffs upon which the Bell farm sits are about 120 feet above the south bank of the Red River. They are made out of limestone, which is quite porous and easily forms caves. Many of the farms in the Red River community, in fact, possessed caves. This one was of considerable size, rising slowly and running back from its mouth at least five hundred feet. It also branches in numerous places. The mouth itself sits a distance above the river banks. During the winter and spring, it is impossible to enter, as the snow melts and spring rains seep through the ground in great quantities and find their quickest route to the river through the many cave chambers, exiting the mouth in torrents.

In front of the cave was a favourite summer fishing and swimming place for the children, and generally when they wanted to get away from the biting insects or when they wanted to eat their lunches out of the sun, they retreated into the mouth. They also used candles to explore beyond the reach of the sunlight. The cave has one large room with a roof about twenty-five feet high. Off of this run passageways.

On this particular day, a boy named Johnny Yoes, who was about nine years old, joined the group. He was quite adventurous for his age, and as he was not an especial friend of Betsy and her normal companions, he was left alone to explore. What he found was a narrow neck, several turns off of the main room. In attempting to rabbit through the small space, he dislodged a quantity of loose soil around him. His candle was extinguished, causing him to cry out in terror. Since I do not believe you have ever been inside a cave, I will tell you two things. The first is that you have never known blackness until all light is quenched inside a cave. Your eyes bulge from your head in the attempt to gather light, but it is useless. Even the most moonless and starless night has some light; a dark cave has absolutely none. Secondly, it is impossible because of the echoes and the many turns and caverns in most caves to tell the origin of an outcry.

Thus was Johnny Yoes in trouble from the moment his candle went out. The other children immediately set off to rescue him but had no idea in which passageway he was lodged. What was worse, his struggles loosened the wet soil and caused more to collapse upon him. With his torso completely covered, no sound could get back to the others. Only by frantic motions of his hands was he able to keep a tunnel open to his mouth and nose.

"Do not make any noise," Betsy called out to the dispersed group. "I can't hear him any more."

"That's because he's buried," Old Kate said, directly behind her. Suddenly, the large room brightened with a soft, white light.

"I'll fetch him out," the spirit voice said. The light moved with assurance up one of the passages.

According to young Mr. Yoes, a pair of very strong hands grabbed him by the ankles and yanked him backwards some dozen feet, well past the collapsed opening. As he was clearing the dirt from his face, Betsy rushed up to him.

"Thanks for saving me," Johnny told her, between tears.

"It wasn't me," Betsy admitted. There was no side passage for more than forty feet behind her. If the rescuer
had been human, she would surely have seen him or her.
Johnny Yoes, however, did not understand the implica-
tion.

"Then who was it?"

"The witch," Betsy said. "You better say nothing about
it to your parents, nor anything about getting stuck, or
none of us will ever be allowed in here again."

Johnny made a solemn promise. It was for naught, as
Old Kate proudly related her noble act at the Bell house
that night. What was more, she visited the Yoes house
and asked if Mrs. Yoes had yet gotten all the mud out of
Johnny's ears, neatly letting the cat out of the bag there,
too.

I have not written about the spirit allowing itself to be
touched, of gathering news for folks, of predicting
weather, of lecturing on theology and singing sweetly, and
of rescuing children merely to fill pages. My purpose was
to show how diligently it worked at being liked. These
kind acts increased greatly after she announced to John
Johnston that she would personally see to John Bell's
death. Supernatural as she might be, she was not unaf-
fected by the animus shown by the entire community once
she issued her fatal decree. This non-human being,
strangely enough, seemed to have the same emotions as
we did, and it could not bear to be hated. Thus did she
work to show her best attributes. Remember that it was
persuaded to shake Calvin Johnston's hand so as not to
be "universally despised." Unfortunately, many who were
not in the Bell family responded favourably to its good
behaviour, encouraging the thing to other like acts. This

evidently gave it the confidence to attack John again and again, with word and deed.

Beyond the very existence of this disembodied entity, its Janus-headed personality was the most perplexing and vexing aspect to deal with. Tuck these good acts away in your mind for when you come to the end of this tale; they all have a bearing.

When I discussed my thoughts with Rev. Fort, he wondered aloud if another purpose of the spirit's kindnesses was to distance us from John Bell. By this he meant that the continuous display of a good side to the creature might lead people to ask if indeed such a benevolent being's hatred of John was somehow justified. Sugg was of a mind that the Devil was certainly clever enough to perform such a ruse and always anxious to set Christian men against each other.

It seemed to me that the spirit craved most, even beyond that of Lucy Bell, the approbation of John Bell, Jr. He and it had a special dance going between them, partly, I thought, out of a mutual respect. As soon as John had returned from his abortive attempt to settle up the North Carolina estate, he put his mind hard to figuring out the demon's methods and intents, especially why it was so hard on his father and younger sister yet so solicitous of him and his mother. Sometimes he would ignore its words with a studied ennui. Other times, he would vigorously engage with it in clever repartee. His most common strategem was to attempt to shame it for picking on a young and defenseless girl. I myself witnessed one such session.

"What do you think of your chances of harming Betsy while I was around if you were flesh and blood?" John Jr. demanded.

"But I am not, so why worry about it?" riposted the spirit.

"What you are for certain is a coward," John shot back. "I have no fear of cowards, being flesh or spirit. If you want a triumph, take me on and let the little girl alone."

"She is not a little girl."

"I will face you no matter what advantages you possess, because I have no fear of you. Do you think I have fear?"

"No, John, I do not."

"You could destroy me on this spot and I would not care."

"What pleasure would that give me?"

"What pleasure can the torment of a child give you?"

"Betsy is not a little girl and no longer a child."

"But she is half my size. If you will pledge to leave her, Drewry, and Father alone you may kill me right now. I care not, for I expect salvation the next minute. What are seven or seventy years on this earth compared with eternity with my Lord? You, however, if you are not already doomed, are sealing your eternal fate in fiery Hell for ever."

I sat in abject awe, afraid to draw even a good breath for fear of disturbing this magnificent confrontation. In spite of being unable to see the spirit, I knew nonetheless that neither it nor John was aware of any of the spectators, so intent were they on each other's words.

"I will tell you something plain and true, Young John: I do not myself know why I can not strike you. I suppose it is your bold daring. Perhaps I do not simply because I know I can hurt you far more by striking your father, Drewry, or Betsy while you must look on in helpless rage.

Moreover, it would give you pride and pleasure to be able to shoulder their pain."

"But why inflict pain on any one?" John cried out.

A prodigious sigh sounded in the room. "There is much I long to say, but it is not possible. I long to speak to some one of great intelligence who is not of this place, so that I might be understood. I am unhappy being here. I was not made for happiness and have no expectation of ever feeling it. Do you not think that I desire to be happy and that I wish to be well thought of? It is not to be."

Despite another half hour of reasoning and cajoling, John, Jr. could not make the spirit reveal any more about the strange mysteries and paradoxes of its being.

On another similar occasion, when John was seeking to protect your mother and to take her punishment upon himself, the spirit took a different and yet an old tack.

"If you truly seek that Betsy is not made unhappy, you will see that she never marries Joshua Gardner," it said, in a low and harsh voice.

"And why do you oppose their marriage?" John Jr. demanded.

"That is not for me to say. What I will promise you is that she will never be happy if that union takes place."

"So you threaten her."

"I have not said so. I have said that you are capable of influencing her. While you may not be able to prevent me from striking her, yet you can spare her pain far beyond that of an open hand on flesh. I have never spoken a lie to you, Young John. Take this not as doing my bidding, for I know you hate me and will do nothing I suggest unless you also believe it in your heart. Take this as you would my advice on harvesting tobacco or saving young people from falling trees."

Much as he loathed the spirit, this once its words struck true, to both his heart and his mind. Soon after, he took Betsy aside and threw his opinion in with that of the "witch," exhorting his sister to heed its words. To his surprise, Betsy promised faithfully that she would not entertain any pleas on Josh Gardner's part for them to become engaged.

By the summer of 1820, word had spread far beyond the borders of our county concerning "the Bell witch" (which was what every one from beyond Red River was calling the spirit). Just as joys and sorrows seem to happen in groups during life, so did a number of studied (I hesitate to say learned) investigations concerning the spirit. Fortunately for the Bells, the summer and fall of that year were excellent for growing, so that they had plenty of fruits and vegetables and fat cows and hogs to feed the hordes that descended upon the farm, ostensibly to help.

Before the summer infestation, one of the savants who visited was in fact invited at John Bell's request. The nicer the spirit became to guests and members of the family, the more venomously it treated John. Usually the voice was that of Black Dog, and it came out with such an intensity of hissing that one could envision a forked tongue behind it. It vilified John and uttered strings of adjectives such as "sneaky, two-faced, sanctimonious, treacherous," followed by nouns better left unwritten. Never, however, would it specify the reasons for its unceasing calumny. Sometimes, this would be done at full voice, with many as witnesses. More often than not it happened when John was alone. On these occasions, John swore that the words were twice as scorching. Usually, the curses were accompanied by sensations in John's

103

arms, legs, and buttocks of pins pricking him. If it happened that he was, at these times, suffering from his lingual and facial attacks, the spirit would openly rejoice and wish John's pain doubled.

From these unceasing assaults upon his mind and his body John began to feel his life's strength ebbing away. For the first time, in early June of 1820, he felt as if the creature was truly capable of making good on its stated goal of killing him. Thus, he was compelled to desperate measures.

For many months, various visitors had been recommending the services of a man who called himself Dr. Mize. This person lived near Franklin, Kentucky, at about the distance of a day's leisurely ride. People credited him with being variously a wizard, conjurer, magician, and necromancer. To John, this all smacked of ungodly behaviour and, in fact, more in league with the Devil. It was his boon friend James Johnston who argued that if this thinking were true, what harm would it do to try to fight fire with fire? Finally, fear and exhaustion wore John down, so that he let Mr. Johnston travel north, accompanied by Drewry, to fetch this putative sorcerer.

This trip was made in the strictest of secrecy, with only the three men knowing their intentions. James and Drewry arose after two o'clock in the morning (the time by which the spirit had always quit the Bell farm), walked horses quietly out of the stable, and saddled them only when they had reached the Brown's Ford-Springfield Road. Drewry had prepared his absence by announcing to the servants and the other members of the family that he had promised to accompany Mr. Johnston soon on a business trip. I had not even heard this much. In truth, I had by this time lost Betsy as a student and so was no longer getting daily intelligence on the doings of either the family or the spirit.

The "witch" showed up at the Bell house fairly early on the morning of Drewry's departure. It droned on with its usual prattle, alternating gossip with vicious verbal barbs at John, until halfway through breakfast. Suddenly, in a surprised voice, it asked why Drewry was not at the table. One after the other, the Bells denied knowing anything about his disappearance.

"That is not possible," said Mathematics, who was the logician manifestation within the spirit. "If you all did know nothing, you would be frantic at his absence by now. You are up to something against me, and I will find it out soon enough."

Many times before this, John Bell had been sure that the spirit had not had supernatural powers beyond its invisibility and had simply crept up on persons discussing secret information and later passed it on, being careful to steer the conversation to the subject it wanted to excel in and then letting fall its wondrous news. John confided in me that he could not believe God would let a demon of Satan have the power to read men's minds. Therefore, since only John, Drewry, and James Johnston had cooked up this trip one night, whilst the "witch" was busy entertaining strangers, and since the other two were now safely away on the road, there was no means by which the "witch" could divine their combined intent.

Nevertheless, that very evening, with myself as one in attendance, the spirit made itself known in the Bell parlour.

"I know it all!" Cypocryphy crowed to all assembled. "I found Drew and Old Sugar Mouth twenty miles northeast of here. I followed along beside them invisible for a couple of miles, and then I made myself look like a poor rabbit and hopped into the road ahead of them.

" 'I'd shoot it for supper, except it looks too sick,' Drew says to Old Sugar Mouth.

" 'It would be a waste of a bullet if you tried, son,' says the old boy back. 'That's no ordinary rabbit; that's Old Kate in disguise. She's found us.' "

The spirit got to laughing so much, it was quite a while before it could continue, and by then it had infected some of the hearers, so that a general mirth broke the rest of the telling into pieces.

" 'Well, then don't say anything else,' Drewry told Old Sugar Mouth," the spirit reported. Then, to further entertain its audience, it resorted to a close vocal approximation of James Johnston.

" 'Prove it's your witch, Drew. Get down off your horse and walk over to it. It looks tired and anxious for attention. If it lets you carry it in your lap, you'll know it's Old Kate for sure!'

" 'And you can shake its paw.'

" 'Why should I?'

" 'Because every one in the Johnston family seems to want to shake Old Kate's hand. And even if it is only a rabbit, rubbin' its foot will bring you some luck.' "

This conversation was confirmed by the two the following evening. According to Mr. Johnston, he had only been joking about the rabbit being the "witch." His surprise (and Drew's as well) was enormous when he heard about the spirit's reporting.

"When Drewry saw that rabbit, he made Old Sugar Mouth keep his sugar lips shut, but neither one had to tell me nothing," the voice of Cypocryphy bragged to us. "I knew they were on the way to fetch Dr. Mize."

A day after this, I resumed my discussion with John Bell as to whether or not the spirit could read minds. At this point, he was no longer certain. I assured him that his original thinking was probably correct. Once the spirit found them within fifteen miles of Franklin (that being the next town on the road), it had only to reflect on all the previous conversations James Johnston had had with John, begging to be allowed to fetch the wizard. These, the spirit could easily have overheard without having made its presence known. The only surprising fact, which we added to all the others we had noted, was the breadth of the spirit's knowledge of the local geography.

The petitioning of Dr. Mize was successful. James reported that, contrary to all the glowing reports of his eagerness to battle any evil spirit for a price, the man was rather diffident about taking on Old Kate once he had heard the whole story. He had admitted that he had heard half a dozen accounts already, some of them (such as one in which the "witch" had walked directly through the wall of a house, set every candle ablaze at once, herself turned into a fireball and shot up the chimney like fireworks) so outlandish that he had assumed this was a Robertson County contest to see who could invent the most outrageous tall tale about "a colourful haint." After he was assured of the facts by both a Bell son and a next-door neighbour, he indicated that he would be willing to investigate. His courage plucked up enough towards the end of the interview that he reckoned in spite of never having faced anything quite so formidable he wouldn't have any problem exorcizing it.

The much-lauded Dr. Solomon Mize arrived at the Bell farm ten days later, laden down with arcane paraphernalia. He was a corpulent little man, who wore a black frock coat that was a size too large for him and a broad-brimmed hat that cast a shadow over his bearded face. As he had been spotted by one of the Forts at a considerable distance from the Bell farm, a goodly gathering was in attendance upon his arrival. This seemed to delight and hearten the fellow.

Swinging down from his saddle, Dr. Mize announced that he was humbled by the calling and deadly serious about his task of removing Kate Batts's spell. With a blizzard of self-congratulatory words, he promised to disclose the precise incantation that had manifested her curse and then use holy rites to banish the demon back to the Hell it deserved. Some were delighted and impressed by the bluster and pomposity, but John Sr., John Jr., and I were crestfallen after the first minute.

Nevertheless, as with every other guest before him, Dr. Mize was welcomed into the Bell home. He, in fact, was told by John Sr. that he had "the place of honour" (which of course it was not) in the upstairs hallway, as this was the place from where one could most quickly reach any "witch" disturbance, no matter where it occurred in the house.

Dr. Mize had no sooner laid out his sleeping and personal gear than he set about erecting strange pieces of equipment. One, for example, which looked like the sort of toy wooden windmill the Germans display at Christmas, was supposed to disclose the passing of the spirit. It was so sensitive that the slightest movement in a room, either by breeze or person, set it going, which made it of dubious value. Also, from an expensive box of polished hardwood he produced different-hued liquids inside tubes, which were purported to change colour if the witch were present. These never worked.

For three days and nights Dr. Mize poked around the house and the out-houses, seeing and hearing nothing. He assured us that this was not uncommon, as spirits recognized his powerful aura and skulked away. Sometimes, he claimed, just the threat of his presence frightened away the ghost for ever. No one in the community believed this would happen with Old Kate, despite the fact that it had almost never been absent for so long and that it had never shown fear of speaking with any one.

On his second evening, after ten o'clock, Dr. Mize shooed every one from the parlour. The Bells reported that he could be heard reciting incantations, and on the morrow powder marks were found on the floorboards that indicated he had created some sort of magic circle. This, of course, did not succeed either.

The third day, the sorcerer burned various pungent mixtures in the house and recited passages from the Bible. He found a shotgun which no longer worked and proclaimed that the "witch" had hexed it. If nothing else, Dr. Mize was clever with his hands. He disassembled the weapon, cleaned it, and rebuilt it, whereupon it worked to perfection. This and the spirit's continued silence gave him great confidence that he had succeeded in his calling (the agreed fee to be paid upon success I never learned).

Whilst the quiet hours passed, Dr. Mize heard from family and friends the most minute details of the haunting. In return, he regaled us with tales of similar events throughout the world. For a time, I wondered if these were not as contrived by the exorcist as his windmills and tubes. Later, as I will relate, at least two of them were corroborated by another visitor.

The first concerned a vagrant drummer in England by the name of Drury who was sentenced for publick drunkenness and noise making by a certain magistrate, and his drum confiscated. Drury was not long in gaol [sic]. When he was let out, he made much complaint about having lost his drum. The magistrate went off to London on business, and no sooner had he done so than his family heard rappings on their doors and tappings upon their windows, as well as what sounded like the roll of a drum. Try as they might, they never caught any one lurking around the house. The drummer, naturally, was suspected, but he could not be found. The magistrate broke the drum into pieces, yet the noises persisted. Soon, other objects such as shoes and chairs began flying around inside his house. Chamber pots were found overturned upon beds. His children, two girls of about ten and twelve, were lifted into the air by an invisible force.

This magistrate had powerful acquaintances, so that after the haunting went on several months he was able to petition from the king several learned advisors. One of these was supposedly the great architect Sir Christopher Wren. These men dutifully recorded the supernatural happenings but were not able to do anything to stop them. One advisor was sleeping upstairs in the magistrate's house when he heard a rapping at his chamber door.

"In the name of God, what are you and what do you want?" this man cried out.

"Nothing to do with you," said a voice that was unlike any one's inside the house that night.

One time, when the magistrate had finally been driven

to desperation, he fired with a pistol upon a moving piece of wood floating in the air. It dropped to the floor. When he examined it, he found drops of blood.

Finally, Drury the drummer was located. He had been boasting in taverns that the haunting in the magistrate's house had been his doing, as he had fixed a curse upon the place. According to Dr. Mize, the man was tried for witchcraft and banished to a far-away colony of England.

The second tale concerned a young French girl who was the servant in a minor noble household and about fourteen years of age. She was the nanny of a tiny baby and was one day rocking the child's cradle when the armoire sprang open of its own accord and began emptying itself of clothing. In the coming months, she had baskets overturn on her head, loaves of bread tumble from shelves upon her, and even harness wrap itself around her in the stable. When a priest attempted an exorcism, he was shaken up and down until his spectacles broke. Even though the supernatural events always happened in the girl's presence, when she was dismissed from the house they continued. Finally, another exorcism succeeded in casting out the spirit.

The third story came from the time of Increase Mather. Some place in New Hampshire, a man named Walton had a house. Just after he and his family went to bed, they were aroused by the sounds of rocks hitting the roof and walls. Although Mr. Walton went outside he could find no person near his house, and yet the stones continued to fall.

Here again, the mysterious events went on with no logical answer for so long that it attracted the attention of official personages. The secretary for this colony came to investigate and was struck down by several good-sized rocks and stones. His report was that the source was supernatural.

Dr. Mize's final story mightily astonished the hearers, because it involved no less great personages than the Wesleys, from whom Methodism sprang. John Wesley and his brothers were away at boarding school when the haunting began, but his father, Rev. Samuel Wesley, his mother, and his sisters were all under the rectory roof.

The trouble began with knocking on the doors and walls. Some times there are boring beetles that live in English houses and make knocking noises. These are called Death's Head beetles and are thought by many to raise a racket when some one in the family is about to die. The house was thoroughly investigated, and no such infestation was found. Soon after were heard footsteps on the ceilings, glass shattering in the windows, and great metallic dins as if someone were emptying buckets of coins upon the floor, none of which truly happened. Later, the rustling of silk was heard in the hallways, as if a ghostly woman were walking up and down.

As with John Bell, some in his community did not like Rev. Wesley. According to Dr. Mize, some of these persons had hated him so that they killed his farmyard animals and even set his former house on fire. Consequently, a close watch was placed on the outside of the rectory. No one was ever found lurking around. What was more, and again as with the Bell troubles, the noises had begun on the outside of the house but quickly moved inside, where no stranger could have ventured undiscovered.

Another item that rivaled the Bell haunting was that the spirit seemed to harbour a particular animus toward Rev. Wesley. When he sat down to eat, his plate would skid across the table, out of his reach. Once, he felt a distinct kick in his posterior.

Another similarity was that Samuel Wesley's wife and daughters claimed to have seen overlarge badgers and a white rabbit near to the house, behaving very strangely.

The most chilling parallel to our troubles was the fact that almost all the strange happenings occurred around the presence of a Wesley daughter. Her name was Hetty, and she was nineteen. This haunting, however, lasted only two months.

Dr. Mize was careful to point out that such creatures as these were not like ghosts. Ghosts were often seen, all be it in a foggy manner. Ghosts also seemed to walk the earth because of their own trouble and only frightened the living by accident. Their purpose was not to torment human beings. Old Kate and every other spirit in Dr. Mize's stories made bothersome noises. They also began on the outside of the house and moved inside later. They also all had the ability to move objects, which they often hurled with force. In one of his cases, the creature had the ability to speak. But most interesting was that every incident he knew of involved a female who was no longer a child but also not yet a fully mature woman. In his opinion, the flow of blood that signalled a female's ability to create new life contained enough energy to call up a mischievous demon in a kind of supernatural birth.

These intelligences instilled in me a new respect for Dr. Mize. They certainly made as much sense as anything we in Red River had pieced together. And then Dr. Mize lost the respect he had earned.

On the fourth evening of his stay, Old Kate suddenly appeared right behind the little fellow, uttering a large "boo." For all his weight, Dr. Mize seemed to jump two feet straight up from his seat.

"Dr. Mize, is it?" Black Dog said. "And you claim to be a conjurer."

The would-be wizard sprang out of the seat with his eyes bulging from their sockets. It was as if no one had ever prepared him for the spirit. He spun around in a tight circle, staring in every corner of the room.

"Where are you?"

"I am every where. Just as I am every thing. And what are you? Are you truly a conjurer?"

Dr. Mize swallowed hard and addressed the air. "What business are my affairs to you?"

"What am I?"

"You are said to be a witch."

"And I have overheard you telling many that you are an exorcizor of witches. Does that not make you my affair?"

"Perhaps."

"By whose authority do you cast out demons?" demanded Jerusalem.

"Now who is that?" Dr. Mize asked Lucy Bell, who had to remind him of the spirit's numerous voices.

"By whose authority?" the spirit repeated.

"By the ancient rituals passed down since the time of Solomon."

"I thought you were Solomon," it said, then laughed so loudly the walls shook.

"I mean the great Hebrew king," Mize said.

"No demons can be cast out except by the name of Jesus Christ, the living Son of God the Father."

"I rely on the Lord and his Bible," said Mize. "I also have spells, incantations, and potions."

"Do not bother with the Bible. Better men than you have tried that already. And I have smelt your incense and your potions," Black Dog said. "You have mixed them incorrectly, and you have left out critical ingredients."

"What ingredients?" asked Dr. Mize, continuing to turn round and round.

"If you were a nigger witch doctor you would know how to mix up a potion and spray it in the air so that you could see my shape. But you turn and turn, like a dog getting ready to sleep."

Roundly insulted, the little man drew himself up and set his jaw. "So, you know both about being a demon and spells to get rid of demons?"

"Of course, you stupid dog dropping, you uncooked sausage. Have not hundreds better than you strived to move me from where I choose to abide? Have I not heard all the spells in my centuries of life? Where in your mixtures are black bones and honey, where the fly pulp, the blind-worm blood, even tobacco, which you could pluck right outside the door? Where are your knots? Your bell, book, and candle?[18] Why call me a witch if you think I don't know all the charms? Why don't you get that blunderbuss and blow the room apart with it, you rotting heap of donkey meat? Then I'll give your fat bottom a ride on my foot."

The spirit went on and on, without pause for breath, for several minutes. Its curses and insults built to an intensity that surpassed even the worst it had heaped upon John Bell. Dr. Mize became white as bed linens. He hurried through the front door and out into the darkness and did not return until after the other visitors had left, found him on the track to the main road, and informed him that Old Kate had departed for the night.

On the next morning, Dr. Mize arose early and began packing. He told John Bell that the "witch" knew so much more about witchcraft and exorcism than he that it was useless to try to force it from the farm. When he mounted his horse, the animal bucked and reared and would not be guided toward the main road. With that, one of Old Kate's voices called out.

"Do you need help, oh honourable Doctor? Let me give your horse a slap and send her quickly on her way. And maybe I'll come along with you a piece."

The horse let out a whinny and then bolted off at top speed. The doctor was seen still hanging on for dear life as his horse dashed across Red River, headed hotly for Kentucky.

That evening, Old Kate bragged in the Bells' parlour precisely how she had tormented the old man all the way home. Some days later, it was carried back to us that Dr. Mize was telling essentially the same story.

Only a few days after this, a gentleman arrived from England. He called himself Edmund Wharton, but I discovered quite by accident that this was not his real name. My thinking (and that of a few others) was that he was a relative of the Bells whom they had written to about the troubles the year before. He had deigned to cross the Atlantic to help but wished to keep his family name as distant as possible from such a scandalous affair as was raging in the wilderness of Tennessee. He did not bother to disguise his accent, and while I have never been to England, I should think from having heard numerous people of various regions of that great nation that he hailed from somewhere around Surrey. This I never

Dr. Mize's horse bucks as the Bell Witch helps the "witch layer" flee Red River with haste.

learned, nor his real name. At any rate, he was treated especially cordially by the Bells and seemed to have more than a passing interest in the events. He also had more knowledge of other such hauntings than I suspect a normal Englishman would. He it was who told us more about the two English hauntings to which Dr. Mize had alluded.

The first, about the drummer, had taken place in a town called Tedworth some two hundred years ago. The spirit linked to the Wesley family, he shared, was called either the Epworth ghost, after the name of the rectory, or else Old Jeffrey, the name given to it by the Wesley children. Also, Old Jeffrey apparently wanted to speak but could only make garbled sounds and groans.

This Englishman, who I must say was one of the most learned and articulate fellows I have ever met, stayed for more than a month and kept a quiet presence during his time in the Bell house. Old Kate noted him soon after he arrived and asked what he wanted.

"I want nothing. I am just a visitor. You need have no fear of me," said "Mr. Wharton."

Curiously, the spirit accepted him at his word. None among those friends who knew that Wharton was not the man's true name had the cheek to ask Old Kate to betray his secret. If she knew his true identity, she did not bother sharing it with any of us. I, for one, held the greatest hope in this smart fellow unlocking the spirit's secrets, but he merely sat observing, day after day and night after night, smoking his pipe with a look of mild amusement, and after about six weeks, without offering his opinion of the phenomenon in publick, he also went on his way.

Old Kate seemed fond of showing off for this gentleman. I suppose it was because he never seemed shocked by any of her displays. For him she invented a new game, which was balancing items upon each other in impossible towers. When he shared with us his extra intelligence about the Tedworth and Epworth ghosts, Mathematics jumped in with her own story.

"I know about a ghost," she said. "There once was a girl who was poor but very vain about her looks. Every time she stooped by the pond to haul up water, she gazed at her image for many minutes. This did not please her enough, though, as it was not perfect in its reflection of her beauty. She bothered and bothered her parents for a mirror, and they were sore pressed to afford it. But since she was so beautiful they could deny her nothing, even though they starved. For her twelfth birthday she got her mirror. Her father hung it on her bedroom wall as a surprise.

"When the girl saw it from a distance, she became very excited. Before she would look at herself, she put on her only good dress. She brushed her long hair a hundred times and tied colourful ribbons in it. Then she stepped to the mirror.

"She was very pleased to see that her beauty was even greater than she thought. But then she saw another face in the mirror, just over her right shoulder. She turned. There was no one else in the room. She turned back to the mirror. The face was still there, and now even closer. She saw with shock that it was also her face. But it was very pale. It had no animation. The image's eyelids did not blink. Her chest did not rise and fall. She was looking at her 'fetch.'

"When her parents came into her room to see how she liked their gift, they found her stone dead on the floor."

There was a silence in the room. And then the English gentleman spoke.

"I've heard it before," he said. "But with tedious and needless detail."

"When I want to detail a haint story," Mathematics replied, "I do it personally."

"We do it personally," Black Dog corrected. Then the four voices of the spirit began singing salty ballads.

During Mr. Wharton's stay, the Bells received the attentions of another investigator. This one they had not invited. He called himself Mr. Williams and claimed to be a "detective." None of us had heard the word before, but he assured us that it had recently been coined in France and was rapidly becoming an exalted profession. Now, of course, the term is better known. His very use of this new word so awed the Bells that they agreed to let him investigate to his heart's content.

Mr. Williams told us that he had heard of the Bell troubles all the way from Baltimore and that he had journeyed out to Red River at his earliest opportunity. He was not in the least shy about his thoughts. Straight out, he declared that he wanted to increase his reputation as a detective by solving the Bell mystery. Furthermore, he said that there was no such thing as preternatural or supernatural events, and that he would get to the bottom with a logical explanation. This fellow had such a bluff way about him and John Bell was by this time so desperate that he was invited to stay and "detect" for as long as he wanted.

Many of the women in the neighbourhood thought Mr. Williams cut a fine figure in his eastern clothes. He was certainly not so rotund as Dr. Mize had been. But he was to my way of thinking well filled out. Nor was he as taciturn as Mr. Wharton. Rather, he blew his trumpet more than Dr. Mize ever had, but he went on continually with such marvelous personal detective stories that several of those most involved in the Bell misery began to think that finally the man to solve the mystery had arrived.

Just as it had with Dr. Mize, Old Kate kept perfectly quiet for a time, I believe taking the measure of her opponent. After a day, she made just enough sounds within the walls for Mr. Williams to wonder aloud if all our concerted uproar had been caused by mere mice. Mr. Williams had attracted quite a daily following with his scientific searching. Each time a strange noise occurred, it was near a member of the family.

The detective had evidently not believed us when we told him how playful Old Kate was. Clearly, he took her bait and thought the Bells were combining to make a fool of him. We learned the depth of his true thinking about the "Bell witch" when he went out on a walk and came across myself and James Johnston conversing near the school house.

"You should think twice about keeping these Bells as friends," he counseled James and me.

We asked him the reason.

"It is exactly as I suspected. They are all in league together to create this silly witch."

"For what purpose?" James demanded.

"Why to make a fortune, of course."

It did no good for us to explain how John Bell had taken the burden of feeding at no charge every man who came to his farm to witness the spirit, either invited or not, and that perfect strangers such as himself were made welcome under the Bell roof.

"It's false charity," Williams countered, "calculated to make them seem all the greater victims. You'll see what they ask when some one wants to publish their story. I have found nothing because there is nothing to find."

We told him that we had personally seen and heard marvels that defied natural explanation.

"Then you are either part of the scheme or else easily fooled," he told us. "They are afraid to do more than make timid noises when I am in the house, because my skills would expose them in a minute."

I had expected nothing from this man. Knowing already that he would never be able to prove the spirit was a human prank, I had long ago dismissed him. Therefore, I was neither greatly put out nor surprised by his opinion. Mr. Johnston, however, took considerable offense at his words and went straightaway to John Bell, to recommend that Williams be ridden out of Red River on a rail. This conversation was held inside one of the barns.

Unlike the detective, Old Kate lived up to her claims, including the ability to be in many places at once. Neither James nor John was very surprised when her voice sounded in their ears.

"Don't do nothing, John. You leave this impostor to me. I will soon show him just what I am made of, and you will see that he is not very smart at all."

This pleased John, because at least for a while Old Kate would focus her wrath away from him and onto this blustery city man. I did not go over to the farm house that night. James must have told many people in the community that Old Kate had vowed to teach this detective a lesson, however, and the parlour was crowded. A good social time was had, but the spirit neither spoke nor made any of its usual noises the entire evening. Mr. Williams took more courage from this, saying that as long as he was in the house whatever was causing the disturbance would not have the temerity to make a display.

Normally, the local visitors would wend their way home by nine o'clock. This night, though, many held on to hope that Old Kate was yet fixing a mighty show and so were loath to leave. Lucy and Betsy dragged out the straw mattresses and laid them in the parlour and dining room. In the center of one arrangement was Mr. Williams. All the lights were snuffed. Gradually, every one drifted off to sleep.

Towards midnight, Mr. Williams was awakened by a great mass pressing upon his chest and stomach. He cried out, more in annoyance than fear, and called for candles to be lit, to expose the human culprit.

In the darkness, this was more easily asked than granted. Whilst people roused themselves and attempted to shrug off their torpor, Williams began to shout in earnest, begging for help. It seemed that his arms had been pinioned above both sides of his head and his face was being punched and scratched.

"So, Mr. Detective," Old Kate said in his ear, "which of the Bells do you think is on top of you?"

Before Williams could answer, he was again pummeled about the face. According to the others in the room, it took little more than a minute to light a candle. The moment its beams fell upon the man, the weight came off him and the punching and scratching stopped.

Williams sat up with a start, sucking down air for all he was worth. He glowered at every one in the room, clearly believing that they had conspired to fall upon him in the darkness and then feign innocence. He might have held to his conviction, had the voice of Old Kate not again sounded in his ear.

"Don't go blaming them," the spirit whispered.

Mr. Williams jumped up with a shriek. The others backed away, not wanting to inherit any of the abuse Old Kate might care to add to his punishment.

"Now go sit in that chair like a good boy and maybe I won't knock your head off," it told him. He did just that, and clutched a candle holder with a lit taper the rest of the night, quaking like a birch tree. Every few minutes, the spirit would whisper in his ear, taunting and reviling him.

With the first rays of dawn, Williams was out to the stable and away from the farm. Those who had seen him after the attack said he was the most frightened individual they had ever laid eyes on.

Finally, no less a personage than Andrew Jackson, the greatest of Tennessee's sons, visited the Bell farm. At this time he was still basking in the glory of his Alabama, Florida, and Louisiana war victories and had not yet allowed his friends in Nashville to promote him for the first time for the presidency.

Old Hickory was no stranger to Robertson County nor even the Red River area. He was a personal friend of the Forts, the patriarch William in particular, from their days in Nashville. He also knew John Jr. by name, as your uncle had volunteered in Springfield when Andy Jackson made the call to oppose the Creeks and the British. John Jr. served off and on with Jackson, from the Indian campaigns to the rout of the Red Coats at New Orleans. This was how he became such a crack marksman, since he had so much practice shooting at targets, most of which were at the same time shooting back!

Unfortunately, John Jr. was not at home when Jackson arrived, as the general had given the family no notice of his intent to visit. The general was nonetheless very welcome, for finally there would be a witness who had a national reputation and who had even served in both houses of the United States Congress. If Old Kate was kind enough to entertain him and he carried the story around, strangers would be compelled to believe the truth of it.

As world distances go, the stretch from Nashville to Red River is not much. By late summer of 1820, the word of the "Bell witch" had spread well beyond middle Tennessee, and the Bells had already played host to several parties from Nashville. General Jackson came north with six men friends and also one unsavory fellow whose name I neglected to record. I saw all of them only from a distance, but this one character was clearly less refined than the other men, wearing backwoods clothes and sporting hair to his shoulders that might never have known soap. The reason I only saw him from a distance was that so many had crowded the Bell farm after learning of the great Jackson's arrival that I thought to give him a little breathing room and to meet him later. You see, the word came to me as I looked from afar that his plans were to stay a full week. Unfortunately for me, this was not to be.

All of what follows came to me second-hand, but it came from so many sources, including your grandmother and mother, that I can not but take it as gospel. It seemed that General Jackson had heard of the constant press of visitors to the farm and so had thoughtfully brought his own wagon filled with tents and camping gear. He rode with his friends behind this wagon. Naturally, they came up through Springfield on the main road. When they were within a mile or so of the farm, they anticipated with excitement the prospect of meeting a real ghost. Two of the men declared that this would soon be proved a tall tale and that they had better think about hunting and fishing to fill their time.

With that, the wagon stopped. This wagon was being pulled by four good horses. Moreover, where it stopped was clear and level ground. The earth was dry and not even badly rutted. The wagoneer laid hard on his reins and coaxed the horses to strain to their limits. The wagon groaned from the stress being placed upon it. And yet it did not move.

General Jackson climbed down from his horse to inspect the wagon. It was his idea that something had gotten stuck in either an axle cradle or perhaps even within the hub of one wheel. He could find nothing wrong. He asked his friends to assist him in lifting each wheel off the ground and proved to himself that it turned without impediment. Then he organized this little army into pushing from sides and rear in tandem with the team of horses. Still, the wagon could not be budged.

General Jackson tossed his hat into the wagon and mopped his forehead with his kerchief. He laughed at the predicament, then said, "What else can it be but the Bell's witch?"

From close by came Old Kate's voice, soft enough that only Jackson and one other man heard it. "I am glad you understand at last, General. Now you can go ahead. I shall speak with you again tonight."

Immediately, the wagon became unstuck. When Old Hickory related the spirit's words to those who had not heard, several scoffed and said that it was only the wind in his ear. The strange business with the wagon and his own words had undoubtedly put the sound of a voice in his head. The second man then wondered aloud why General Jackson's thoughts had also caused him to hear a voice. The gay mood among the party changed, and a couple among them discussed the wisdom of continuing on. But General Jackson laughed all the harder and reminded them that this was exactly what they had come to witness.

The party arrived at the Bell farm not long afterwards. John was, for once, delighted to play host. He announced that General Jackson would have the downstairs bedroom to himself. Jackson declined courteously, stating that he had long ago grown accustomed to tent living. He introduced his friends and then announced that the odd man had been engaged by the party to "lay the witch," as he had made it known in Nashville that he had a considerable talent at such things.

After generously shaking hands and being cordial to nearly every one in Red River, General Jackson retreated to the dining room with his friends and enjoyed "the fatted calf." By the time they had finished, darkness had nearly set in. All who could fit into the parlour and hallway made themselves comfortable. General Jackson was coaxed to recount his memories of John Jr.'s heroisms. Then he was, in turn, regaled with the "witch's" many antics during that summer, especially with self-proclaimed expert witch chasers.

The witch layer evidently took this as a challenge to his presence there and piped up with stories of his many accomplishments in defeating the supernatural. He pulled from his pocket the tail of some poor, dead black cat. This he proclaimed had belonged to the familiar of a witch who had recently been killed and whose grave he sat upon to wait for the cat. When it arrived to mourn for its mistress, he plugged it with a silver bullet. Having said this, the man produced a horse pistol and let every one know that it was again loaded with a silver bullet. He had killed the cat purposely to get its tail, for he said that if he stroked it on his nose it would take on an electric charge. He alone had the power to see this charge, but he assured those gathered that it would take on a bluish hue when a spirit approached. As he spoke, he stroked the tail against his nose.

This seemed to lull the hearers into a silence of expectation. Not willing to relinquish the floor once he had gotten it, this man began to call upon Old Kate, daring her to enter the parlour and face him.

General Jackson was clearly not amused by the bore's soliloquy. He leaned over to his closest friend and whispered, "Did you ever hear such brave words? I bet you that Apollo here is a coward.[19] If for no other reason, I wish the spirit would appear to show this braggart's true colours."

That seemed to be what Old Kate was waiting for. At the next interval of silence, the sounds of footsteps approaching were heard. At first they were light as a young girl's, but rapidly they changed to the tromping of a heavy man's boots.

"General, I am here as I promised and ready for business," Old Kate announced.

Even the great Andrew Jackson was too dumbfounded to answer.

"And that business would be this bag of hot wind," she went on, from directly in front of the witch layer. "With that tail up against your nose, your little, puckered mouth looks like the cat's asshole. I thought it was supposed to warn you when I was near. I've been standing behind you for the past quarter hour, puddin' head."

The man's mouth worked like a fish's out of water, but he said nothing.

"Well, at least shoot me, for Christ's sake. I'll make it easy and stand right in front of you."

Those in the room directly before the man parted like the Red Sea for Moses. With a quaking hand, he raised his pistol and pulled the trigger. The hammer fell, but nothing happened.

"Try again. Hurry up. I can't wait for ever," Kate ordered with a scornful tone.

Again, the pistol failed to fire.

"That was your turn; now it's mine," the voice said.

With that, the man was hauled up from his seat by his nose. She told him to never mind stroking his nose with dead cat, that she would stroke it for him. The group heard several sharp slaps and saw the man fall to the floor. Then he appeared to be forcefully hauled up by his sizable nose, both nostrils flared out as if fingers or claws were shoved inside them. He danced on tiptoes around the room, slapping feebly at the air and screaming that his nose was about to break.

The front door swung open on its own, and the great witch layer was led, squealing like a stuck pig, outside. When he was released, he ran up the track in the direction of the main road. He never did return.

General Jackson had followed the furious demonstration out into the night. It was reported that he laughed so heartily that he had to lower himself to one knee.

"That was the most fun I have had in my life, and I am glad I said nothing against Old Kate," Old Hickory said. "I vow I would rather fight the entire British army single-handed than face this witch."

To this, the spirit said, "I am pleased to entertain you, General. I'll wager that is the last we will see of that coward. But there is another in your company who is a fraud. I will attend to him tomorrow night, as the hour is getting late."

Presently, the Nashville group settled down to sleep. When the morning came, several of that number convinced General Jackson that the "witch" could not possibly top her display of the previous night and that they might as well go on home. The neighbours were more of a mind that each of them privately suspected himself the next object of terror. By mid morning, they were packed and on their way south.

Andy Jackson did not bring any other friends to Red River, as we supposed he might. He also kept mighty close-mouthed about it. Perhaps he believed the stories he had been told about the Bell witch being able to roam the earth and find any one it wanted to bedevil. Then again, it was not too long after his visit that this long haunting came to its horrible end.

In spite of all the merry diversions Old Kate created in punishing those who sought to prove her an invention, a pall hung over the Bell farm because the spirit continued its attacks upon John steadily. Moreover, it was not just John who was gradually being worn down by the spirit, like the hardest stone eroded by a constantly surging river; Lucy also was being worried to frailty. Knowing the creature's oft-stated tenderness toward "Old Luce," John Jr. used one of its nightly appearances to remark on his mother's obvious deterioration. While no amount of argument would turn the spirit from its wrath against

Andrew Jackson

"Old Jack," the son thought that by appealing for Lucy's health he might indirectly make the thing quit in its torment of his father. Old Kate restated her fondness for Lucy but absolutely refused to let up on John Sr. until he was "dead and buried."

In the middle of September Lucy finally fell sick with the pleurisy. Her fever soared, and her coughing became frightful. Dr. Hopson visited twice but was able to offer no remedy. Old Kate appointed herself Lucy's nurse and constant companion. This attention produced the opposite effect from that intended by the spirit, further sapping your grandmother's strength. The spirit could not seem to understand how its presence could be bad. What startled me was that this magical creature, who could be in two places at once, who had the strength to resist horses and men together, who astonished us with the new trick of producing food from thin air, could offer neither medicine nor spell to cure this person she clearly liked. It got me reflecting that calling it a witch was the most ignorant of names. Witches dealt in spells and paid for this power with the forfeit of their immortal souls. Surely such a creature as this should not only have been able to conjure up a mixture or poltice to cure some thing as common as pleurisy. Surely, in fact, if she were a witch she should have been able with a charm of magic words to have made Betsy and Joshua not only fall out of love but to become enemies rather than plead first with me to break them up and then with the lovers themselves. I realized that this being itself was a miracle but was at the same time quite limited in its ability to create miracles.

"Poor Luce, poor Luce," it would lament over and over. "I am so dreadfully sorry that you are sick. What can I do for you, Luce?"

For her husband's sake Lucy bore the attention, although she often told the spirit that she was too weak to speak. Some times, then, it would lapse into silence, but it was clear that at least part of the creature was standing guard all the time. When some one came into the room and looked for medicine or another pillow, Old Kate would immediately chime in with direction or advice.

Often, when your grandmother had neither the strength nor inclination to converse with the spirit, it would offer to sing. This, fortunately, proved as soothing to Lucy as did the nightingale in the fairy tale about the Chinese emperor. And, in truth, the creature did have a lovely singing voice. What was more, it knew more songs and of more divers types than any living person I have ever met. There were many hymns, such as "Ye Followers of the Prince of Peace" and "Adeste Fideles," English ballads like "Barbara Allen" and the "Tobacco's but an Indian Weed," sea chantees such as "South Seas Bound," and, despite its aversion to darkies, even an occasional plantation spiritual. Lucy's favourite was "Come, My Heart," which it sang every day. The lively songs set toes tapping, the ribald ones drew laughter, and the sad ones never failed to fetch a tear from the listeners. These last were the most poignant, as the lack of a physical singer in the bedroom lent a mystical, unearthly nature to the airs.

In spite of all its ministry, the spirit could not rally your grandmother. She sank lower and lower over the span of two weeks, until she lacked even the strength to eat. This, as might be expected, also contributed to the further failure of your grandfather, who did not often sit in the bedroom, as Old Kate could not help hurling imprecations at him even as she attempted to nurse Lucy. Instead, he sat outside the door in a rocking chair John Jr. had newly built, covered with a quilt. He would rock and listen, rock and listen, inquiring of each person who left the bedroom how his wife was.

Each neighbour wife visited in turn, bringing one of her cooking specialties to tempt Lucy into an appetite. None worked. After weeks of this, Old Kate got her own idea.

"You aren't eating because they have brought you what they love to eat and not what you love most," it told Lucy, not caring that it had offended your aunts Martha Bell (whom the spirit always called "Pots") and Esther Porter, who had just arrived with baked breads. "I have observed that your favourites are hazelnuts and grapes."

"Yes, I do love them," Lucy admitted.

"You be patient for one minute. I'll be back directly."

Not much more than the minute passed, and the familiar bodiless voice returned.

"Poor Luce, hold out your hands, and I'll give you something really special."

Lucy did as bid, and from the thin air rained a shower of hazelnuts. Your aunts screamed in shock and ran from the bedroom. John Jr. and Drewry were summoned. They went up on chairs, examined the ceiling above the bed, and found it solid.

"While you are busy doubting me again, your mother is starving to death," said the spirit peevishly. "Why don't you go away and let her eat the nuts?"

"I have nothing to crack them with," Lucy said.

"Is that all that's keeping you? Here, let me attend to them."

With that, Lucy, Drewry, and John Jr. all heard the

distinct crack of nuts. All around the coverlet and even inside Lucy's hands were opened shells.

"There! Now eat!"

"You are so very kind, Kate," said your grandmother, "but I am too weak to chew them."

"Then, here. Grapes are not too hard to chew."

With that, a second shower poured from the ceiling. This time it was plump, individual grapes. Lucy ate a few of these. Perhaps it was the comfort to Lucy's mind provided by such an unselfish show; perhaps the sickness had merely run its course. Whatever the reason, from that point Lucy began to recover and was back on her feet in less than a week.

The word of the spirit's conjuring of hazelnuts and grapes traveled as quickly as if it had turned fishes and loaves into food for five thousand. People who had tired of Old Kate's same patter and antics suddenly were back at the farm, begging her to reproduce the miracle. Equally delighted to have back her audience, Old Kate would drop a bunch of grapes out of the thin air, usually into Betsy's lap. To further ingratiate herself, she told the visitors exactly where in the woods she had found the native treasures of grapes and nuts.

As soon as it was clear that Lucy would survive, Jesse Bell and Bennett Porter moved their households out of Red River. They had had enough of the "witch" and of the bad position they were constantly placed in with people, owing to their fame in being linked to the Bell troubles. Good opportunities for land had arisen in Mississippi, and this was all the excuse they needed. While both Lucy and John gave their blessing and, on the surface, applauded their children's efforts to escape the privations of the "Bell witch," they also felt a bit of abandonment and betrayal, or at least great sorrow at seeing a son and daughter simultaneously disappear in their hours of great need.

I have saved one story out of order because it is so illustrative of the final year of the spirit's haunting. In early February of 1820, a goodly snow had fallen. Then as now, the children were anxious to wring every bit of joy out of it that they could, with snow ball fights, snow forts, and so forth. The Bell farm had a log sledge used for many tasks of heavy transport. It was not the elegant sort of sleigh you see in Springfield these days, but if hitched to a team of horses it could serve good duty to pull the children around the farm to view the fleeting white world. The children of the neighbouring farms all knew of this sledge and came over late in the morning after the snow fall.

The sledge had been used that morning for farm labour and had been unhitched so the horses could be fed. The mass of children, however, were impatient to get the horses back so that they could be off on their sleigh ride. They shouted and hooted at Drewry and John Jr., who were in the barn, to hurry with the horses.

"We don't have to wait for them," came the spirit's voice. "You all hold on tight, because I'll turn some corners."

With that, the sledge started off down the incline. True to the voice's direction, it veered around the house and more than once defied gravity in its snaking course.

The children were only a little nervous by the time John, Jr. and Drewry caught up with the sledge and hitched it to the horses. Most declared that the ride had been the best fun they had had in months. Nevertheless, Betsy got off before the natural part of the ride began. As she walked away, she called back her reason to her inquiring friends.

"I am cold. I have been cold all day, and I do not want any more of this ride."

That incident and your mother's words I believe very nicely summarize the entire year that followed. The thing that most Red River folk had come to call Old Kate with familiarity and, verily, even affection would take them on a gay ride from one winter to the next. She would joke and divert and educate and serve as excellent almanack and save a child and run off frauds and charlatans and sing prettily and nurse and produce food from nowhere, and yet she was also the selfsame supernatural creature that had promised to kill John Bell without offering so much as a motivation. She was the selfsame being that punched and tormented defenseless children. The weather itself and the land conspired to make the year joyous, as the skies were blue except when rain was needed and then it fell in abundance but not too much. The crops, especially corn and tobacco, had never come in so well. The hogs and cattle were fat, and disease among them was unknown. Even the people, notwithstanding the occasional accident or stillbirth, were in exceptional health. Red River might have been called New Eden without fear of contradiction. All in all, from January to November of 1820 it was as delightful to every family as had been that impromptu sleigh ride offered by the "witch." To every family, that is, except the Bells.

For them, 1820 was brutally cold, with never an opportunity to feel warmth. They had been chilled to their hearts all year and wanted no more of this supernatural ride. Unlike the sleigh ride, the spirit offered no opportunity to get off.

October of 1820 came, and with it no surcease from the spirit. The only change seemed to be that the creature had diverted nearly all its abuse of Elizabeth and her brothers to their father. John's face fairly danced hour after hour with contortions. No one in the community had ever personally known such an affliction nor heard tell of any one who had ever had it.[20] This led nearly all to conclude that it was directly brought on by the "witch." Similarly, no one had ever heard tell of a swollen tongue, other than when they had accidentally bitten their own. In such an instance, while one might bite anew the member several times before the swelling subsided, it never lasted more than a few days. Dr. Hopson was brought in for about the fifth time. Once again, he offered a new nostrum for "nerves" but went away without receiving a personal experience of the spirit and so still doubted its existence.

For John Bell, the twitches and swellings had now gone on fiercely for twelve months. John had also begun his seventy-first year (I can scarcely call his seventieth birthday a celebration). It was patent to any one who had been familiar with him in former years that these physical torments had taken a frightful toll, for he was terribly gaunt and hollow-eyed. On the few occasions when he was not plagued for a few days, he would rally and, I believe, endeavour to look more hearty than he truly was. These periods of respite were also times when the witch appeared to have flown off somewhere else to do mischief.

Like a human crutch, Richard Williams became his constant companion and surrogate strength. Your uncle

Richard had by this time reached eight years of age. I must say the events of the previous seasons had made him mature beyond his years. When he walked beside his father, there seemed to be one little old man walking beside another tall one.

The entire month of October, the spirit was present at the farm, concentrating its fury on "Old Jack" as if tiring of the haunting and determined to have it over with as soon as possible. It followed him day and night, inside and outside, cursing with its vile tongues and in its several voices, analyzing John's deterioration with glee, predicting his demise before Christmas. Its displays became so barbarous that your grandmother pleaded with it on her husband's behalf, thinking that if the spirit had been so distraught at her grave illness then perhaps it would love her enough to relent from its deadly purpose towards John. For her troubles, Old Kate turned a deaf ear.

On October 17, which was a Tuesday, John suffered his worst attack to that date. It was so severe that, for a time, we believed he might die straightaway. When it did pass, he was so weakened that he was compelled to remain in bed for an entire week. All this while, the spirit ranted just outside his door, as if to deny him any rest at all.

By the 28th of October, a day that was brisk of air and pleasant to most of the world for its sunlit splendour, John felt recovered enough to venture outside on farm business. The following had no witness other than Richard, but I cannot doubt that it was any less harrowing than his oft repeated descriptions of the event.

John was too light in the head to bend over long, and so had instructed Richard to tie his shoes. These were good shoes, made by a traveling cobbler whose name I forget but who visited Red River a couple of times a year and who made excellent footwear. The family had had the shoes made for John to elevate his spirits, and they fit his feet like two gloves.

Together, John and Richard left the house and started towards the hog pens, which were at the normal distance to keep the odour from the house. According to Richard, his father's purpose was to sight out those hogs ready for fall slaughter. The pair had not gotten even halfway to the pens when one of John's shoes came off his foot. Richard knew he had done a thorough job of the lacing not five minutes before, but he held his tongue, even though he suspected the "witch's" doing. He had his father lean against a fence post while he refitted the shoe and, this time, tied a double knot. They started off again, and pretty soon the other shoe flew off. Both man and boy knew this to be a supernatural occurrence, but each refused to give the tormentor the satisfaction of comment. Richard noted that his father's face had become pale, but John refused to change direction and retreat to the house. Instead, they forged on until they had reached the pens. Richard was sent to fetch the slave men. By the time he returned, his father had determined which hogs were to be butchered. The orders were given, and those doomed were culled.

"I tell you, Richard, I feel like one of them hogs," John confided softly, once they were away from the Negroes and making their laborious way back to the house. "I feel like I have been separated out for my final fate."

Richard was about to refute the lugubrious remark when his father's feet went suddenly out from under him, and he fell hard to the road on his posterior. Richard saw with horror that both his father's feet were up in the air and the shoes were being jerked off, against the tightness of the knots. One shoe went over the fence; the other sailed far down the road. Then John cried out that his face was being struck. He nearly went into a swoon, but Richard was right behind him, holding him up. He manfully helped his father to a log that lay beside the road. Richard asked if he should run for help, but John told him to fetch his shoes and put them back on.

When Richard returned to the log with the shoes, he saw that his father's face was alive with twitching. As he was so young, he had been spared this hideous transformation as much as possible, but now watching it in the full sunlight, he was afraid that his father was turning into a demon before his eyes. John mustered his waning strength and, with a gentle voice, commanded Richard to replace the shoes yet again.

While Richard worked with trembling hands to do the laces up, the air around the road was filled with a raucous loud voice singing "Comin' Through the Rye." It completed one verse, then launched full voiced into a chorus of "As Pants the Hart for Cooling Streams." As soon as it left, yelling an Indian war whoop, John's affliction passed. John, who had ever been a rock to his family and community, began to cry and passed his hands tenderly along Richard's young face.

"Oh, my son, you have been so patient and kind to your father in his need. But you will soon be relieved of your burden, as I will of mine. I can not much longer endure the persecutions of this unspeakable creature. My end is surely near."

Richard protested the words, but John only hugged him to his chest and cried out to heaven, as Jesus had shortly before his death. He asked, if it were possible, that God should relieve him of the torment or at least give him the strength to continue facing it. Failing this, he asked to be forgiven of all his sins and to be taken into the bosom of Abraham. Drawing strength from his faith, he went on petitioning and extolling the Lord until he felt recovered from the shock of the creature's attack. With only a little help from his son, he returned safely to the house.

As soon as John had passed through his front door, he felt immensely tired and took to his bed. He was able to eat and drink a bit and spoke of venturing out again on the morrow. But this was not to be. Through the last days of October and the few days left to him on earth, he never left his house. Old Kate kept visiting, kept up her cursing, singing, and threats of approaching death. John, listening in stony silence, offered no fight. He had clearly been convinced by the spirit that his fate was sealed. His appetite dropped off. Nothing Lucy, John Jr., or any of the other children did could coax him to regain his will to live.

On December 12, the "witch" predicted that John would never see the next sun. A panic gripped the family, made all the worse by the creature's refusal to visit that night. Only the youngest caught any sleep. The sun rose, and John was still with them. That evening, Old Kate roared with laughter over her latest lie, declaring that she had spoken the words purely "to wear the old bastard out with worry," thus hurrying his real final hours.

"Yes, I lied," she told the family. "But this is the God's truth: when the New Year turns, so will John Bell. In his grave."

December 19 dawned a bitter cold day. It is common knowledge that the older a person becomes, the less sleep he needs. As the eldest, John had for years generally been the last in the family to retire and the first to rise. Even during his worst afflictions, he never failed to wake with the rooster. This morning, however, he appeared to be in a sound sleep when Lucy awoke, and so she left him in bed and began her morning ritual. The children performed their early chores whilst Lucy supervised the slaves in readying breakfast. Every one ate. Then the children went out again, to cut evergreen boughs with which to decorate the house, since it was the sixth day before Christmas. It was only then that Lucy returned to her bedroom to see if John had the strength to leave the bed. Never once had it entered her mind that she would not find him alert.

When Lucy approached the bed, she realized that John was in a profound sleep, with none of the stirring associated with that hour. His chest was hardly rising and falling, and those muscles of his face that had so often of late twitched and danced were now completely slack. She called out to her husband in a loud voice. He did not stir. She then put her hand to his neck to feel for a pulse and could barely locate it.

Lucy's repeated calls attracted the attention of John Jr., who went to the three-cornered press in the corner of the room closest to his father's side of the bed. There were kept the many medicines which had over the months been prescribed by Dr. Hopson. John had often been the one to dole out his father's medicines, so he knew every bottle in that cupboard. Thus was he more than surprised to find a semi-transparent bottle of the height of his thumb standing at the front of the collection. Inside, it was about a quarter filled with a black liquid. There was also one drop of the liquid under the bottle when John lifted it, half absorbed into the press's wood, showing that the bottle had been unstopped not long before. No one in the household could say whence the bottle had appeared.

As no one in the family wished to be long removed from their comatose father, I was enlisted to ride to Port Royal to fetch Dr. Hopson. When I arrived there, I found that he was elsewhere making a call, and so I was compelled to wait for the better part of an hour, pacing back and forth.

On the road back to Red River, I confirmed Dr. Hopson's antipathy towards the notion of a supernatural being in residence at the Bell farm. Knowing that I was a close friend he was careful in selecting his words, but he made it clear nonetheless that he thought the entire Bell family were a collection of charlatans and hypochondriacs. He knew nothing of the depth of my education in the matter, but I let him sample it as we rode along, at the same time offering in rational and calm terms my own experience with the spirit, so that he appeared somewhat chastened from his hard opinions by the time we reached the farm. In all, I had been gone about four hours.

When we entered the house, Frank Miles, John Johnston, and Alexander Gunn were there, all looking greatly agitated. These close neighbours had been fetched by the Negroes. Frank, true to his nature, charged into the bedroom and grabbed John halfway out of the bed, shouting at him to wake up and shaking him like a doll.

Dr. Hopson's eyes went wide upon the next words, which were spoken by John Johnston.

"I followed Frank in and was about to exhort him to lay John back gentle on his pillow," Mr. Johnston said, "when the damned witch spoke up, right beside the bed."

"I heard it too, plain as day," chimed in Alex Gooch. "She told Frank it were no use to shake him, as she had finally got Old Jack good, and he was a goner for sure."

John Jr. then asked if his father's condition had anything to do with the strange bottle in the press, and she affirmed that she had brought in a vial of poison during the night and given it to John in his sleep. He had taken more than enough, she crowed, to kill him. With that, she gave out a harsh laugh and vanished, deaf to the men's pleas to return and answer more questions.

John Jr. suggested that they test the contents of the bottle and find if it was indeed poison. Alex Gunn ran out to the barn and captured one of the many cats, by chance a coal black one. Meantime, John Johnston had drawn a straw from a broom and dipped it into the bottle. By this means and by several repetitions, the cat was induced to swallow the liquid. Soon after the dark droplets reached its stomach, the cat began to race around the room, then to weave and whirl as if drunk, and, a few minutes later, to fall over into a stupor. It never moved from where it fell, and in fact was dead about an hour after it had been poisoned.

Dr. Hopson confirmed that John had slipped into a coma and was in a very bad way. He detected an odour upon John's pale lips. He was shown the bottle and stated that it was definitely not one of the several ones he had brought on former visits. He sniffed the vial, first said that it smelt very like the odour emanating from John Bell's mouth, and then said that he could not be sure, since he had very little acquaintance with poison, but that it might be the juice of the black nightshade berry. He set it down to examine John more carefully. In those few moments, and with everyone's eyes fixed on the doctor's

The death scene of John Bell, featuring the poisoning of the black cat

ministrations, Frank took up the bottle and marched it out to the dining room fireplace. I noted the missing man and bottle only moments after he had left the room. Despite my rush to find him, he was already tossing the remaining liquid into the flames.

I gave a shout for Frank to stop, but it was too late. His action had emptied the bottle. Whatever was inside caused the flames to blaze up with a bright blue light. Frank was still confused when I lamented the disappearance of the remaining liquid, so that I was forced to explain that a learned apothecary in a large town like Nashville might have been able to declare with assurance that the black liquid had been extract of nightshade. Thus, if John did die, could murder be firmly fixed as the cause.

Dr. Hopson said that there was nothing he could do to revive John. He felt that any action such as the ministration of a physick to drain away any poison still in his bowel might kill John outright. He declared that the old man's life was out of his hands and suggested that fervent prayer might be his only salvation. Receiving his fee, he took himself home.

The day passed slowly and sadly. John never moved, and appeared all but a gaunt corpse. That he had not long before succumbed, owing to the constant using of energy for his nervous condition and his inability to gain nourishment while his mouth was swollen, is a testament to both his will to live and his superb constitution.

More friends accumulated in the house, and we all took turns on the death watch through the night. Old Kate came and went during that night, like a firefly's tail winking on and off. Each time she made her brief appearance, she would utter some horrible statement such as "Ain't he dead yet?" or sing a snip from a profane song like "The Girl I Left Behind Me."

Early on the morning of Wednesday, December 20, 1820, John Bell breathed his last. The only consolation we could find was that John had finally passed beyond the pale where this earth-bound spirit could get him. If there was any doubt as to the "witch's" purpose in haunting the Bell household, it appeared to be answered when she disappeared all through the time John was laid out in his bed as well as the sizable wake that was thrown. I must say that I have seen many shells of the departed lying in their deathbeds, but never have I seen such a husk. If ever a face was the embodiment of the expression "a haunted look" it was John's. My words are insufficient in this; only a death mask might have told the tale.

The funeral was conducted at the altar of the Bell house, on account of John having been excommunicated from his church. Faithful to their friend to the last, however, the Rev. Sugg Fort and the Revs. James and Thomas Gunn were in attendance and took turns performing the service. The four dozen or so mourners who crowded into the house cast wary eyes about during the entire service, fully expecting Old Kate to dishonour the proceedings with her outrageous words and singing. Once again, we were relieved to find her absent.

I had been one who had volunteered to mattock out the frozen earth in a plot some thousand feet from the house. Dean had appointed himself the melancholy task of fashioning the casket. The pall bearers were Jesse, John Jr., Drewry, John Johnston, Frank Miles, and Bennett Porter. Words were said over the open grave, dried flowers and hair wreaths were dropped onto the box, and the mourners took turns shoveling in the clumpy mounds of dirt until the hole was completely filled.

As the last shovel full was thrown, the female voice of Old Kate could be heard, as from the tree directly above, singing "Row Me Up Some Brandy, Oh" in a drunken voice. We all did our best to ignore her, but she would not be discouraged and followed us back to the house, singing through the boughs. At least she had the decency not to enter the house.

A short while after the burial, we had a deep and very heavy snow. That night, the spirit came quietly to the Bell house, appearing only as a voice. Lucy, Betsy, Joel, and Richard refused to speak with it. Only John Jr., who had so often refrained from intercourse with the demon while his father lived, now deigned to enter into conversation. Without raising his voice or uttering oaths, he petitioned the spirit to finally supply an answer to why it had haunted his father, now that John was dead. Even then, it declined.

"If you truly had a justification why he deserved death," John Jr. said, "why not say it now so that we will no longer love and adore him? Do you not know that the dead are much more beloved than the living, as they can no longer disappoint or inconvenience those who loved them?"

"That notwithstanding," it answered. "But why should you berate me? You have just said that I have made it easier for you to love your father."

"But he can no longer love us. You are the cause of his leaving this earth before his time."

"He can still love you and does," the voice assured him. "He looks down on all of you from heaven. I could say to you that I could conjure up his spirit and then imitate his voice in order to convince you of this, but I do not wish to deceive any of you here."

John Jr. owed that he would not have believed at any rate. The spirit and John spoke of the dead at length, of death itself, of religion, of good and evil, and many deep metaphysical subjects. All the while, John Jr. reminded the creature that, interesting as the discourse might be, he could depend on not one word it uttered. He told me that his plan was at the very least to embarrass it, so that it would either leave them for good or else speak a string of truths about its nature and purpose, to try to force John to believe. Instead, it became angry and indignant.

"You think I could not fool you if I wanted?" it said to John Jr. "Go over to the window." When he had obliged, it said, "Mark you how the snow is pristine. Not one blemish upon its surface. Watch!"

As John looked, footprints advanced from the distance right up to the window.

"Now, take your father's boots which are still inside the chest on the porch and go out to the tracks with them!" it ordered.

"I will do nothing for you," John Jr. replied.

"You already know what you would find; the boots will fit precisely into the tracks. If I had wanted to convince you of a ghostly visit by John Bell, I could have made you believe. I could have had his voice confess to horrible sins. But this was not my purpose here. I will soon bid this house good-bye, and when I do, I will not be heard again for a great long while. Do not worry, then, when you hear a scratching on the roof. It will be a tree branch in the wind. Or a gnawing on the bedpost. This time it will be a mouse. When I have gone, I have gone."

It did not say good-bye forever that night. A few other people in the community professed to hear Old Kate in the days following the snow fall, but all of these were the unreliable types, who would either credit the creaking of a door to the supernatural or else were not above making up tales for the momentary attention it brought them.

Despite the spirit's promise to leave the Bell family in peace, soon after New Year's Day Betsy was overcome by terrible dreams. These, she told her mother, were brought on by her increasing worry that the creature, having killed her father, would concentrate its fury upon her and haunt her to her death. The spirit knew of this conversation and soon afterward visited Betsy while she was in Lucy's presence. Speaking in a gentle voice, it professed to harbour no animosity towards her. It said that, as a proof of this, it would quit the house for at least a week. It kept to its promise, and each day Betsy became more her old self, to the point that she again learned to smile and was even caught humming some of the catchy tunes the spirit had sung.

In truth, your mother became better than her old self. She was now three years older than when the creature had first visited, a woman of fifteen. Childhood charms had given way to womanly beauty. Moreover, the torment of the visiting spirit had deprived her of much of her young innocence and advanced her to an age beyond her years. Worry had melted her baby's fat, causing her figure to be thinner and more womanly than those of her friends. Even her voice had lowered considerably.

All these aspects contributed to my taking of James Byrns's advice. I had lost several pupils to age (Betsy included) and, because of the turmoil so near the school, had not actively promoted myself among the families with younger children. I was getting on in years and had to think of bettering my position. Teaching in a larger community such as Springfield was sure to be a step in that direction. I also felt, as Magistrate Byrns had opined, that my education could strongly benefit my neighbours as their representative in the legislature. But, most compelling, I could no longer stay in the humble school house and watch Betsy grow older and more beautiful, from a place at once so near and yet as distant as a foreign shore. All too soon, I knew, free of the spirit's imprecations, she would renounce her promise to it and wed Joshua Gardner. Although I had been assured I was free to use the school house and adjoining land for as long as I wanted, I had to leave. This I did in the middle of January, 1821.

I established myself in a small house in Springfield and went to work on both my teaching and political careers with a fury. This I suppose was as much to force Betsy out of my thoughts as to advance myself. Whilst I quickly prospered, I was largely unsuccessful at my other purpose.

From time to time, I received reports on Red River, which, of course, is only a couple hours away by horse. From what I heard, the "witch" was becoming weaker and weaker and visiting with less and less frequency. John Johnston could still engage it in sprightly repartee from time to time, and it still criticized the sermons of the Gunns and Sugg Fort, but it had given up chunking rocks at passers by the Bell farm, given up snatching away bed clothes, and even forsworn boxing Drewry and Frank Miles. Most believed that Kate Batts's purpose in calling up the demon had been fulfilled, and it must soon after return to Hell, whence it would emerge upon the earth in some other form to plague mankind. Some believed that the hatred of the community was too much for even its cruel nature to bear. Only John Johnston continued talking nicely to the being. I never questioned him later, but I trust his reason was his unflagging hope that he might cajole or trick the thing into revealing its true nature and origin. The rest of the folk quit laughing at its antics, quit petitioning it and giving it opportunities to cavort and show off. Indeed, even if John had not died, the novelty of the "Bell witch" had already begun to wear off. With John's death, almost no one wished or dared to come to hear it. I am sure that no actor has ever stayed long on the stage once he discovers there is no audience beyond the foot lights. So it seemed to be with Old Kate. Even her voice had lost its clarion tones.

The old hens who professed to hear Old Kate all around Red River directly after John Bell's death were no doubt the same ones who spread tales of the "witch" and Betsy becoming bosom friends once John died. Your mother later assured me this was all nonsense, as she never quit being frightened to the point of speechlessness around the thing that had not only so tormented and abused her but which also had killed her beloved father. Nonetheless, stories went out that the spirit completely changed its nature towards her and treated her with especial tenderness. It would often, they said, counsel Lucy to "take great care of your noble girl." According to them, it brought her delicacies to eat from foreign lands and sat with her by the hour telling the news of the great and famous in countries all around the world. The news, of course, turned out to be absolute fact in every case.

Spring of 1821 came. With it came the time when all pupils were released to help with farm and trade work, leaving me free to campaign until the summer school session. If I was to win, I knew that I would have to encourage the vote of every man I had ever come in contact with from Red River to Port Royal. On the Saturday before Easter, I set out in that direction. I worked my way northwards but slowly, visiting every home in my path and taking time to admire the rhododendron, cherry trees, and azaleas in bloom. I did not arrive at Red River until Monday, on account of being obliged to observe the solemnity of Easter Sunday.

When I reached the Johnston lands, I was informed that Joshua Gardner had formally proposed to Betsy on the previous morning, and she had accepted. To seal his pledge he had given her a beautiful engagement ring with an emerald stone.[21] I was' also informed that, on account of every one having Easter Monday off to jubilee, the darkies included, most of the community would be down by the banks of the Red River. Most assuredly, there would be one party of three young couples pick-nicking at Brown's Ford. These would be my protégés, Theny Thorn and Alex Gooch, Rebecca Porter (with her swain James Long), and Betsy Bell and Joshua Gardner. Surely, I would want to visit with them.

Having received this news, I knew that there was no means to avoid these couples without directly offending many people. I rode up to the ford, passing by the extensive Bell pear and peach orchards, which were abloom in dainty hues of white and pink. I thought briefly to stop by the school house and see if it was empty or was being used to gainful employ, but my heart was not in it.

When I reached Brown's Ford, I observed that far more than three couples were reveling there. Perhaps a quarter of the entire community could be spied up and down this winding stretch of the river. Some young men were playing mumblety-peg with knives. One slightly older was carving his and his lover's initials into a stout tree trunk. The ladies and girls were mostly engaged in picking jack-in-the-pulpits, celandine poppies, tiny irises, wild columbine, and other spring blossoms.

The object of my hunt was Betsy. I found her amongst her closest companions at the very spring where the spirit had convinced Drewry, Bennett, and "Old Sugar Mouth" Johnston to dig for treasure. The great, flat rock had not been moved back to its original position. I remember having thought at the time that this could serve as a symbol; I believed that because of the spirit's haunting, the entire community would never return to the original paradise it had been.

When I was spotted, a general whoop went up, and I was crowded round. The younger men remarked on the especial daintiness of my canvassing clothes and proposed to "bring you down off your high horse" by throwing me in the water.

Theny, always the most vocal among the young ladies, scolded the boys loudly and drove them back with a stick. After she was reproached for being too serious, I was assured that those men old enough to vote had even before my visit determined to cast in my favour. Further, as soon as word came up from Springfield of my candidacy, they had all begun "stumping on Professor Powell's behalf."

Whilst every one was congratulating me and predicting an easy win, I was studying Joshua Gardner. He was now fully grown, a man of twenty-one years and ready to begin a family. He was at that pinnacle of power when one first turns from adolescence to manhood and he was, moreover, a handsome creature. When one added in his

Richard Powell, depicted in his "stumping clothes"

ready wit, his prosperous and respected family, and his unwavering devotion to Betsy, there was no doubt in my mind why she had accepted his proposal.

I confessed to the gathering that I had heard already the news of the betrothal. Betsy was called forward through the crowd to display her ring. I admired it. I also inquired if Josh intended to settle in the area. He replied with a smile that he would remain in Red River long enough to give me his vote, but that his plan was to move himself and his bride due west in the near future, to newly opened territory nearer the Mississippi River. This would be more than a hundred miles distant. My heart grew heavy, expecting never again to see Betsy after that.

Your mother was resplendent that day, as I suppose all young women who are newly affianced must be. The difference was that she started with a natural beauty that beggared other young women. And, of course, that I loved her. She cunningly wore a dark green dress that emphasized the color of the stone on her finger. A cascade of thin green ribbons streamed down from her golden hair. She looked to me like the very goddess of spring.

The time to dig up worms for bait had come. The men took up their spades and buckets and headed for the damp soil. I, meantime, found an opportunity to draw Betsy aside, into an overgrown cranny in the steep bank, where no one was likely to chance.

"I hardly know where to begin in what I wish to tell you," I confessed to my beloved.

She blushed and cast her eyes downwards. "I must be very vain and proud to think that you might speak of your love for me."

"Beyond love," I answered. "I adore you and would

require hours to tell you why. Has not your mother spoken to you of my abiding affections?"

"She has, on a few occasions. But you are far too grand and learned a man for such a simple girl."

I stepped behind Betsy, which compelled her to turn. My intent was to keep one eye on the entrance to our private place. I do not recall precisely the arguments I gave her for changing her mind, but she was implacable. She asked me why I had not spoken up for myself before this, and I gave as excuse our relationship as teacher and pupil. She reminded me that her mother and father had decided she had had enough schooling soon after her fourteenth birthday, and that she had not been my pupil for some months before I left for Springfield. In all that time, why had I not taken her aside as I did now? I answered that, during the deepest sorrows of her family, with first her mother and then her father gravely ill, and then her brother and sister moving away, the time was hardly right for proposing to take her away from them as well. Even Joshua had refrained from paying amatory visits, I pointed out. I used her question to my own advantage, stating that it proved she cared for me and had been awaiting my suit. This she denied, although she professed to be infinitely fond of me. Finally, she held her ring up before my eyes and said that her pledge had been made and could not be unmade on any account. Joshua was too fine a man to deserve anything less than complete loyalty.

I knew I was defeated. I took her raised left hand in mine and lightly kissed it. I asked if the nuptial day had been set. Betsy shook her head.

"Will you come to my wedding if I invite you?" she asked.

I could deny her nothing. "Yes, Betsy, if you wish it. Only please, do not ask me to give you away in your father's place."

"John will do that," she said, then looked anxiously over her shoulder.

I knew that we had stolen too much time away and quickly led her back out onto the river bank. We walked side by side for a while, reminding me painfully of a similar walk I had taken with Lucy Bell, when she beseeched me to marry Betsy and carry her away from Red River.

All too soon, Joshua appeared. I handed Betsy over to him and climbed up to where I had tethered my horse, waving to every one I passed, putting on a brave smile.

I rode directly north across Brown's Ford to canvass those of the Fort clan not celebrating by the river, so the rest of the day's uncanny events had to be related to me. In fact, I heard them from no fewer than half a dozen tongues. No two stories agreed in every detail, but enough of them bore the following threads so that I may rely upon them to weave a strong pattern of truth.

As soon as I had taken my leave, Betsy grew contemplative. She did not yet appear sad, but her mood was noted as being much more placid than the others around her, who were diverting themselves with shouting, the spraying of water at each other, and by wading in the river. Some of the older folk were in fact quite annoyed that the fish were not biting on account of the noise and the disturbed waters. All this while, Betsy sat apart, on a grassy knoll overlooking the river.

The servants of the various families had very early in the morning claimed their fishing spots as a body, upstream of Brown's Ford. One of the most outspoken of the tribe was Uncle Zeke, the patriarch darkie of Thomas

Gunn. Whilst their masters' frolicking was at its highest pitch, he came down the bank and proclaimed to the gathering that "de Indian spirit be here" (he had grabbed on to Old Kate's first lie and stubbornly refused to consider any other source of the haunting). With eyes large as tea saucers, he declared that he had felt its presence strongly.

Frank Miles roundly cursed out Zeke a moment later. Among his more gentlemanly words, he accused the African of being "an ignorant old savage," first because the spirit had not been heard in Red River for almost a month (by far the longest stretch since its first appearance), and second because Zeke's words had dredged up all the memories of dread in the Bell family and those close to it, like "a hail storm out of the blue heavens."

Zeke had just turned to retreat when one of Josh Gardner's fishing lines was seized by a monstrous fish. So great was the creature's weight and strength that the pole was yanked out of the mud. Pole, line, cork, and hook were carried at a brisk pace upstream until finally the whole affair got tangled in with other lines. The fish used the tension to work itself loose.

As Josh set about disentangling his pole and line, Frank pronounced the fish to be a prize-winning trout. Others speculated that it was a great eel. Zeke, not cowed by the imprecations earlier heaped upon him, affirmed that this was the physical manifestation of the spirit, just as it had been known to inhabit dogs and turkeys and rabbits.

Despite her distance from the bank, the loudness of all these speeches had carried to Betsy. Hearing the talk of the spirit, she lost the last vestiges of her gaiety. Josh, alert to her mood, climbed up and attempted to assure her. But Betsy would not be comforted. She, too, she revealed, had a sense that something unnatural was about to happen. She urged Josh to return to the banks with the others and try to catch a glimpse of the thing that had taken his hook, to prove that it was nothing more than a large fish. He would not leave her side.

A sudden cool breeze blew towards the river from the direction of the Bell farm. Heads went up from the suddenness of it. Dialogues stopped. A curious hush came upon the gathering, such as will happen once or twice at a party in the course of an evening, perhaps when a clock tolls out the hour. Upon the unexpected zephyr floated a small but distinct voice.

"Please, Betsy Bell, don't have Joshua Gardner!" The familiar tones of the "witch" echoed over the water.

Those few who had not yet stopped talking fell swiftly silent. Every one turned as one body and looked at a place beyond where Betsy sat.

"Please, Betsy Bell, don't have Joshua Gardner!" it implored again.

Betsy's mouth dropped open. She clapped her hands over her lips and stared at her betrothed.

"Please, Betsy Bell," said the voice a third time, in its most plaintive tone, "don't have Joshua Gardner!" And then it was gone.

In the hours that followed, I was told, a few suspected that it was myself, hidden among the trees, feigning the voice of the dread spirit, driven to a desperate gambit at separating the young lovers by my own love for Elizabeth Bell. To my credit, few entertained this wild surmise. At any rate, it was later proven that I had already reached the Fort settlement by that time.

As the throng waited with bated breaths for the spirit to speak again, Betsy's eyes began to stream with tears.

As she had done on the pick-nick when Josh had first announced their engagement and the spirit had spoken, she jumped up and ran south towards the Bell house. Once again, she was closely followed by Joshua.

Joshua managed to halt her flight at the head of the spring and persuaded her to stop and take a cooling drink, since she looked very flushed. She cupped her hands and sipped some water, then allowed Josh to daub at her forehead and brow with his moistened handkerchief. It was at this selfsame place and time that she told him she could not go forward with the wedding. The "witch's" prolonged silence had given her the hope that she might at last be free to marry Josh, but its reappearance with the sole purpose of deploring the union proved it was never far away. It was clear to Betsy that the being had come to Red River for two purposes. The first was to kill her father, which it had accomplished in its own slow time. The second was to see that she never married Joshua Gardner, no matter how long that might take. Neither made sense, but that had no bearing upon the fury of a creature that, by all lights, also made no sense. The only possible chance that Betsy could see for making the spirit depart for ever was to recant her promise to Joshua, out loud and for all time.

If my fervent arguments to Betsy only an hour or so before could serve as the yardstick, I am sure that Joshua spoke with intense passion and urgent eloquence to turn Betsy's mind back towards their marriage. There may have been shouting with his reasoning, and tears as well. But Betsy would not be moved from her conviction. Even if he did succeed in wedding her and taking her west, she stated, neither of them would ever have a minute of true peace. Silence proved nothing. The witch had sat at two

162

church services simultaneously, and no one had an inkling of its presence. A force beyond that of nature had set itself between Betsy Bell and her young lover, and that was that.

At length, Joshua was compelled to yield to Betsy's conviction. He bade her keep the ring, but she could not. Out loud, to the witnessing wind, birds, stones, flowers, and, she was sure, the unseeable "witch," she swore on the sacred memory of her father that she would never wed Joshua Gardner.

That evening, when Betsy was alone in her bed, the spirit's voice whispered to her that it was at last content. It promised that it would soon bother the Bell family no more, although it did reserve the right to drop in on them in a span of several years. Betsy did not answer.

Within a space of weeks, Joshua Gardner had settled his affairs in Red River and moved west. Having turned his back so swiftly and well, he was wise never so much as to write to your mother.

There were a number of weddings in Red River in the following months, including both couples who had accompanied Betsy and Joshua on that fateful Easter Monday. But Betsy became an old maid. Due to the press of my businesses in Springfield and canvassing every spare moment, I had no occasion to visit that area again until after I had won the election. My curiosity got the better of me in early December, and I knew that I had best go while the weather was with me.

I found the Bell household in fine health and prosperity. All were still in mourning for husband and father and particularly solemn at this time, as the anniversary of John's death was imminent. Betsy was just as beautiful as ever. I thought that she might have regained her old spunk, such as the ways she had in school of imitating what and how her elders spoke, but she had no such diversion to offer. It was as if the spirit had permanently stolen some of her spark. She told me of her plans to stay at home for at least two more years, helping her mother, who by this time was fifty-one. At the end of that period Joel, the youngest of your uncles, would be ten and almost a man.

I was told of the spirit's final visit, which occurred not long after Betsy's solemn promise not to wed Joshua. It came while the family was gathered around the fire place after their evening meal. A rumbling presaged the appearance out of the social room chimney of something like a cannon ball. It was black, but no one could tell by looking if it was solid or not as it rolled a little way beyond the hearth.

Before any one could rise to investigate, Old Kate's voice called out, "You are at last free of me. I am going now. Good-bye to all."

With that, the ball burst into smoke and filtered back up the chimney. True to its word, it has not appeared to the Bells since.

All during this story, I could not keep my eyes off your mother. I lacked the courage to speak to her directly about suitors. Instead, I got Lucy alone later. She said that Betsy would not consider entertaining gentlemen callers, but she also expressed pleasure at my continued interest in her daughter. Although Lucy had said that her husband had been enthusiastic about the notion of having me for a son-in-law, I was never convinced. He never spoke directly to me of giving Betsy away nor made me feel he wanted Richard Powell as part of his family. I thought that this was understandable. His one other daughter, your aunt Esther, had already married. This left only Betsy to care for John and Lucy in their old age. He must have known that, owing to Betsy's great beauty, she would not forever be tied to the farm. Nevertheless I am sure he wished to do everything reasonable to forestall that day. I asked that Lucy write to me as soon as Betsy gave any indication that she was again prepared for courting.

I visited the Bell farm several times in the following years, with no greater frequency than my visits to the Forts or Johnstons. Although I never spoke to Betsy of my continued ardour, I made it known nonetheless by bringing her sacred offerings of books as well as lace, ribbons, and other profane fripperies from my trips to Nashville and Atlanta. Owing to the spirit's supernatural gifts of foods, I was careful never to bring fruits or nuts. Each gift was received with delight and thanks, but she refused my tentative offers even so much as to walk alone together.

Finally, the year 1823 arrived. In early June came the long-expected note from Lucy Bell, speaking of Betsy in terms that gave me courage to resume my pursuit. I felt like Jacob at the end of his long wait for Rachel. Also like Jacob, I had not idled whilst waiting. I still held my post in the state legislature and was prominent on several committees. At the same time I had honestly used my increasing connections to build a modest fortune. I went to Betsy as accomplished as any man in Robertson County. On a Sunday, June 15, I took myself to Red River Baptist Church with my horse and rig. Betsy was there with her mother, as I expected. Owing to the commotion that all my former friends made, she could hardly have missed my arrival. To my delight, she approached me and bade me sit beside her during the service. I could hardly concentrate on Sugg Fort's sermon, which I am convinced he embellished for my benefit, waving his poor rheumatic hands as if the heavenly dove had suddenly descended upon him. After the service, I asked if I might carry Betsy home, and she accepted.

I was invited to dinner at the Bell home that day. Following the meal, I once again asked if she would stroll with me. This time I was not refused. Betsy and I ambled past the old building where she had been my pupil. We walked all through the farm's extensive orchards but avoided the banks of the Red River where the "witch" had twice spoken out against her marriage to Joshua Gardner. For a time, I entertained Betsy with talk of the politics in Murfreesboro, working up my courage. I took her hand in mine, and she did not pull away.

Betsy asked me about the newspaper I had pressed into Rev. Fort's hand as we were filing out of the church. I told her it was an abolitionist piece printed by one Elihu Embree out of Jonesboro, which he called "The Emancipator." Sugg had long preached against the villainous practice of slavery, and I thought he would delight in seeing that a Tennesseean had the pluck to oppose it in print. Betsy had rarely spoken about slavery in general or the Negroes on her farm in specific while I taught at the school. I was surprised, therefore, to hear her offer the opinion that it would be just to free all black persons, provided they would agree to return to Africa and that they themselves should first earn their passages back. It was certainly not the most unkind thing I had ever heard regarding the black man, but I was nonetheless struck by the fact that it seemed harsh and unfair for my sweet Betsy.

I thought no more about the subject, however, when Betsy turned at the end of the orchard row and looked up at me with her blue eyes wide open.

"Have you something to ask me, Mr. Powell?" she asked.

"I would like to court you," I stammered, as one of my own students might.

"Is that all," she asked, offering me the ghost of her old, mischievous smile, "seeing as you already have my hand?"

"Well, it is marriage to you that I desire," I said. "If you will consider my proposal, I am willing to wait a few more years. Or, if you are ready now, I am prepared to marry you today."

Betsy laughed. "You truly are a politician, Mr. Powell! Shall we be engaged this day and set the wedding a year from now, so that I may be sure my mother and brothers are properly cared for, and so that you may have time to repent of your rash proposal?"

I protested that it was not at all rash, but your mother merely went up on her tippy toes and laid a gentle kiss upon my cheek. When we returned to the Bell house and made our announcement, we were met with unmitigated well-wishing. Lucy in particular seemed deeply pleased.

The year went more quickly than I would have expected, and we were married at Red River Baptist Church with much ado and merriment. As the spirit had been absent for more than a year, no one spoke of it at the celebration, but I am sure that more than myself had their minds distracted by (illogical as this phrase may be) its lingering shadow.

Betsy moved directly to Springfield and into this house, which I had had built according to her wishes. Your birth

167

marked precisely the passage of another year. Other than her normal period of confinement when you were in your mother's womb, she made herself very active in the social, religious, and philanthropic life of Springfield, being the model politician's wife. I credit her with a large part in my attaining the offices of sheriff and state senator. While others in town society thought her the most ebullient creature in the state, I who had known her in her formative years realized that some of her spark had indeed been stolen, never to return.

Twelve years passed quickly, with every one offering its own special joys. As each year rolled out, we counted ourselves lucky that we had been visited by no great troubles or sorrows to balance against our good fortune. Occasionally, your mother would be vexed by some thoughtless person who would stop her in the street and pester her about details of the "Bell witch." Other than that, as far as I knew she had no outward reminders of the one terrible period of her life. Our greatest joy, of course, has been to see you growing so beautifully towards womanhood.

Then, five months ago, just when you reached the age your mother had been when the Bell family haunting started, our joy was threatened. It was on a night when I was pondering a civic problem that would have tested the wisdom of Solomon. Try as I might, I was unable to sleep. Your mother slept but lightly, aware as she always is of my unrest. In order to give her peace, I determined to move to the guest bedroom. No sooner had I closed our bedroom door and begun easing myself down the hallway so as to soften the creaking of the floor boards than I heard the noise of what sounded like a rock being thrown against the roof. I moved to the staircase window.

Although the moon was gibbous in a sky very lightly clouded, I could spy no one in the back yard. A few moments later, I heard again the clear noise of a hard object landing upon the roof.

I returned to the bedroom to see if the noises had awakened your mother. She was tossing fitfully, but her eyes were closed. I could not see clearly, but they even seemed to be squeezed hard shut. I reconsidered sleeping in the guest room, as I did not want Betsy to awaken to the strange sounds and also to find herself alone. I eased back into the bed and was relieved to hear no more noises. I must have listened for the better part of an hour, but only silence reigned on our property until sleep claimed me.

The next night, the very same civic problem had me tossing in bed. Once again, to spare your mother I determined to quit the bedroom. No sooner had I closed the door to our room when I again heard the sound of stones against the roof. This time I was not so long frozen but rushed straight to the window. Just as I arrived, one of the glass panes resounded. The window frame shook slightly, and yet I had seen no object nor even the shadow of an object striking it.

A moment later, I heard cats fighting in the back yard and rumblings as of approaching thunder. All of these I had heard before. With my heart beating wildly, I felt my way down the stairs and out the back door. I was not surprised to find no cats in sight. The sky was cloudless, with the moon nearly full.

I returned to my bedroom. Again your mother remained asleep, but fitfully. This time, when I lay back down, all the noises did not immediately cease. The cats' jammer and the rumble of thunder lapsed, but an animal of perhaps the size and weight of a bobcat seemed to be pacing back and forth along the length of the roof. This continued until, I estimated, two o'clock.

At first I just lay listening and tried to command my heart to stop pounding. Then I began to work on the mystery. As John Bell had first thought, I suspected some one of executing a prank. This made even more sense than John's surmise, moreover, as literally hundreds of persons knew the history of the "Bell witch" haunting, and their most reasonable means of tormenting my family would have been in imitation. Also, as a politician and former sheriff, I had created far more enemies than John possibly could have. Even so, I knew this could not be the case. I had a clear view of the entire back yard when the window was struck, and no one stood there. Perhaps out in the country, where the Bell farm house lay, someone might have paraded across the roof ridge unobserved, but such mischief would have been folly in the middle of Springfield.

My second thought was that the spirit had finally returned. If this was the case, then the object of the all-seeing creature was none other than myself, since it was my rising that had set off the noises on both occasions. I wondered why it had not started straight out speaking to me but thought that perhaps, after such a long absence, it must be "born" again. The other explanation was that it favoured slow torture and always presaged its eventual speech with a display of brute noises. Whatever the case, I was not about to sit by as a helpless victim, as the entire Bell family had, while it grew again to full power.

During the entire course of the Bell farm haunting, I had harboured a private opinion that Betsy held more of the truth of the spirit's origin and purpose than she told. This was why the creature had punished her so. Other than my one early and abortive interrogation of Betsy I had never said anything, as it was not my place as an outsider. What was more, if I had voiced my opinion, many might have misconstrued my words into an accusation. This was farthest from my mind. I had been convinced over and over again during those years that Betsy had no control over the demon's antics. Yet I believe I several times caught a look in her eyes seeming to say she felt she deserved the spirit's fury.

It occurred to me that the secrets Betsy "knew" might only be known to her inner mind, the part that comes alive while one sleeps and which recasts and reinterprets the waking world through dreams. The main clew to this was the strange fact of Betsy's fits while the spirit was growing and the fact that it never spoke while she was unconscious. My suspicion was that it invaded her body, drew physical strength from her and, at the same time, searched her mind for knowledge of the area, its history, and its inhabitants, particularly of the Bell family. What it might have left behind in exchange was the object of my pursuit.

Perhaps a year before this, I had read a story of one of the revered Benj. Franklin's more remarkable adventures whilst serving as this nation's ambassador to the French court. Around this scant intelligence I fixed my hopes of salvation for the Powell family. Although the next session of the state congress was not to begin for a few days, I made various excuses to your mother to take myself to Nashville early. There, I visited that which pretended to be a public library, as well as the private book collections of several of the town's most educated citizens, with the intent of uncovering knowledge to finally put the "Bell witch" on the defensive.

Here is the information I assembled. Dr. Franklin, as you know, was the prover of the fact that lightning and electricity are one and the same. His recommendation that lightning rods be placed atop all tall structures has saved countless buildings and lives. The Royal Academy of Sciences bestowed their highest honours upon him, and even the king of France sent him personal thanks. Shortly after we had won our independence from Great Britain and while Dr. Franklin was still in France, the ill-fated King Louis XVI invited him to be part of a learned investigation of one Dr. Mesmer.

Franz Anton Mesmer was born in Austria in the first half of the last century. He had received his medical degree from the University of Vienna. He was not, however, content to practice with the truths revealed by scientific observation but had also studied such mystical ancients as Paracelsus, Galen, and King Pyrrhus of Epirus, and also the seventeenth-century Irish magistrate Valentine Greatrakes. He came to believe in an imperceptible healing power that could be radiated from his hands, which he called "animal magnetism." For this, he was branded a sorcerer and banished from Austria. He resettled in Paris, where he found many patients who embraced his theories and professed cures through them. The Parisian community of traditional scientists and physicians, however, were determined to make him prove his strange skills.

The French government appointed a commission from among these men to investigate Mesmer's claims. Because Dr. Franklin had expressed an open-minded view, neither outright condemnation nor gullible belief in Dr. Mesmer's claims, he was asked to join the commission.[22] The work I read said that Franklin had observed the existence of a class of people who seemed to enjoy ill health but who could be convinced to give up their placebos purely by the persuasive charms of a trusted healer. Mesmer seemed to do just this, all be it through the ministrations of a French doctor, since he could not obtain license to practice in Paris. What Mesmer had taught this man to do was to move an iron wand back and forth before the patient, speaking in soft, oft-repeated words as to the healing effects the patient could expect. More than a few patients seemed cured, but when the investigators themselves sat for sessions they proclaimed to feel nothing of Mesmer's "animal magnetism." Dr. Franklin and the rest of the commission ascribed the healings as a certain appeal to susceptible minds. Realizing the damage being caused to his reputation, Mesmer retired to private life in Versailles and later moved to Switzerland.

This information I had originally received with a detached interest and might never have thought of it in connection with our problem except I had also learned that Mesmer had left behind two fanatical disciples among the French nobility. These were the Marquis de Puysegur and his brother, who was a count. These gentlemen discovered that the slow, periodic waving of an object such as a shiny wand, a pocket watch or a golden locket in front of the eyes put many people, patients or not, into a kind of waking sleep. Whilst in this sleep, the people would reply to personal questions they never would answer in a normal waking state. What was more, if they were told they could accomplish some task they willingly accepted the notion, be it even such a silly and embarrassing thing

173

as trying to lay an egg. This discovery both explained how some one who only imagined sickness could be ridded of it instantly and also that Dr. Franklin's surmise about Mesmer reaching into the mind was correct.

At once dubious and hopeful, I approached several friends in Nashville with this news and proposed that we experiment upon each other to see if it worked. I myself could not be induced to this "waking sleep" state; nor could four of my compatriots. To my amazement, however, one friend was indeed, as the report had called it, "Mesmerized" by my watch swinging at the end of my fob chain. He readily answered personal questions and performed acts beneath his normal dignity.

I rushed back to Springfield with my new-found talent and immediately set a plan in motion. I am sure you remember the time that Amanda White invited you to spend the night at her house. I had asked her father to put the idea in Amanda's head, so that your mother and I might have a night completely alone. It was on that same night that I approached your mother with what I called "the new parlour trick imported from Paris, France, and being performed in smart salons from Boston to Richmond." Being ever open to social diversions, Betsy became a willing subject for my swinging watch.

The person in Nashville who succumbed to Mesmerism did so only after considerable trial; in contrast, your mother's eyes began lowering before my little pendulum had described a dozen arcs. What was more, she seemed in a far deeper type of sleep than the gentleman had been. Against the hope that my experiment might work, I had gathered foolscap, pen, and ink, and these I fetched in no time into the living room. Already on the sheets of paper, I had written several questions. I learned, among the night's other astonishing revelations, that a person in such a state is exceedingly patient, as if time is not passing for her. Therefore, one can take the time to write down answers without fear of the subject bolting off in a pique. I laboured to set down both my questions and her answers precisely, although I have omitted those times when your mother's hesitation or too soft replies necessitated a repetition of words.

Knowing so little about Mesmerism and its power, I thought it best to ease into the questioning, as one would entering very cold water, for if Betsy's mind indeed held truths about the demon, the dredging up of these memories might be more of a shock to her than to me. I began by asking her name, where she lived, and details of recent events. This took several minutes. Then I began in earnest:

"Have you lately heard strange noises around the house at night?"

"Yes."

"What kind of noises have you heard?"

"Rocks."

"Rocks do not make noises of themselves, Betsy."

"Rocks against the roof and walls."

"Have you heard other noises as well?"

"Animals."

"Animals such as cats and dogs?"

"Yes."

"What were they doing?"

"Fighting."

"And walking back and forth on the roof?"

"Yes."

"Were these real animals?"

"No."

"How do you know?"

(This question I could not get her to answer.)

"Who made these noises?"

"The witch."

"The same witch that haunted the Bell farm?"

"Yes."

"Is it in this room now?"

"Yes."

"Can you see it?"

"No."

"Then how do you know it is in this room?"

"I feel it."

"Where is it, Betsy?"

"With me."

"Inside you?"

"Yes."

"Can you make it come out and speak with me?"

"No."

"Can it speak if it wants to?"

"I don't know."

"Why has the witch returned after all these years?"

"To protect Missy."

I must pause here and say that the mention of our pet name for you was the last answer I had expected. I required a moment to recover my shock. Your mother sat patiently, with an unfurrowed brow, as she would while waiting for the rig to be fetched from the carriage house. I persevered:

"Why does Missy need protecting?"

"She is pretty. She is twelve."

"But is she not quite safe here in Springfield and inside our home?"

"She is not safe from her father."

176

I experienced no greater shock than this all evening. I felt as if I had been struck between the eyes by one of the demon's invisible missiles. You of all people know that I would be the last one on earth to cause you harm. I am equally sure your mother would attest the same, at least while she is awake. Therefore, I believed her answer contained another meaning. Despite the assault of these words upon my ears, I perceived that Betsy had not spoken of me by name or by saying "She is not safe from you." At the same time, I guessed that she spoke truthfully and that her words were being chosen with great care. If this were the case, the confluence of circumstances that had resummoned the spirit included your gender, your beauty, your age, and the fact that you had your father living under the same roof with you.

Like a shower of shooting stars falling out of a heaven of fixed, bright points, old facts I held as unrelated events and details suddenly rushed upon my conscious mind. John Bell had been considerably older than Lucy Williams when he married her. Lucy was twelve at that time. When his second daughter attained that age, despite approaching his seventieth birthday John was still a potent man. This was proven by the births of Richard and Joel not long before. Although worn by her pioneer life and the bearing and raising of seven children, Lucy held enough of the vestiges of physical beauty in her fifties to prove that she must have been almost as pretty as Betsy when she was twelve. With the assurance of his mortality staring at him in the mirror every day, John Bell may have reflected back often upon his happiest days of youth, vigor, and lust with his young bride. The other constant mirror was Betsy. If, earlier than the fall of 1817, he had been aroused to relive his meanest passions via his younger daughter he was prevented by the fact that Betsy and Esther occupied the same bedroom. Then Esther married Bennett Porter in late July of that year and moved out of the Bell house. Being at the same time such a God-fearing, Christian man, the forces of Good and Evil might have waged war within John for months. I thought this because there were many days between July 24 and Christmas, and it was not until around Christmas that the noises began.

Knowing so little of the power of Mesmerism, I was determined to speak carefully, not knowing the extent of the damage I might cause to your mother's mind:

"Did the witch come to Red River to protect you, Betsy?"

"Yes."

"Did it protect you by making noises?"

"Yes."

"To frighten someone away?"

"Yes."

"To frighten your father away from your room at night?"

"Yes."

"Did it protect you the first time your father came to visit?"

Your mother opened her mouth to answer. Her lips and jaws worked, labouring to produce a reply. What came instead were two great tears from her eyes.

When I first wrote down this next part, I merely summarized it, on account of your tender age. Since God has seen fit to keep me alive despite my stroke these six years, you have in this time grown to full womanhood. You often wondered aloud how I was whiling away my hours in the study, and I was frequently evasive. The fact is that

I twice expanded this account. The next passages provide minute and, I believe, vital details to the story. Nevertheless, prepare yourself for brutalities that no proper woman should ever be required to read. Keep in mind, however, that your poor mother lived through this. Also, any physician or theologian to whom you show these pages is also entitled to a setting down as precisely as I am able, in order the better to help your mother and any other unfortunate woman who may similarly suffer.

I repeated the question: "Did it protect you the first time your father came to visit?"

The voice that answered, from the opposite side of the room, I had not heard for many years. Yet it was frighteningly familiar. It was the boyish voice of Jerusalem:

"So, you have finally guessed our secret."

Naturally, my first reaction was to start half way out of my seat. I mastered my astonishment as best I could. "I have guessed that John Bell stole into Betsy's room on several occasions," I answered with evasion, since I did not possess the spirit's secret in any way. "He always went to bed after all the others, and so it was no great matter that he would be afoot near midnight."

"He came into her bedroom and slowly pulled the bed covers off of poor Betsy's beautiful body."

"Is that where you got the idea to pull everyone's bed clothes away?" I asked.

"We did it to mock John Bell. To let him know that we had watched what he did. That we had witnessed his unspeakable sin."

"But you did not protect Betsy the first time he visited."

"No. He had his filthy way with poor Betsy. He moved his hands up and down her sides so slyly. Can you bear

179

to hear this about your wife, Dick Powell, or should we go away?"

"I can bear anything, if it is the truth," I said.

"This is the truth. At last, poor Betsy was awakened by his touch. It was black as sin in her room, so that she could not see who was taking such audacious liberties with her. She opened her mouth to scream. He clapped his big, hard hand over her mouth and stopped up the sound. At the same time, he whispered to her who he was and that she had no reason for fear. She relaxed. Shall we go on?"

"Yes," I said.

"Old Jack Bell told poor Betsy that she was his beloved daughter, and that he would never hurt her. All he wished to do was to make her feel good. To feel pleasures she had never felt before. Poor Betsy held still while he put his cracked, old lips upon her soft, ruby ones. He was her father, but she knew even at that tender age that such kisses are reserved for lovers. She attempted to squirm away, but he pinned her with his weight. Then his hands began to lift her night dress.

"Poor Betsy opened her mouth again to scream. This time, Old Jack's one hand went up to her lips and the other one went around her throat. He clamped hard. So hard that poor Betsy could not get her breath. She thrashed and kicked."

"Just as she did every night with her fits," I remembered. "She was reliving her terror right before her guilty father's eyes."

"Just so. And then Old Jack got very angry. He hissed to poor Betsy that his visit was all her fault. Surely he was not to blame that she had grown into such a beauty, beyond his endurance to resist. Her charms were unnat-

180

ural. The very Devil had given them to her, to tempt him. Well, he would fuck the Devil right out of her!"

"He did say those very words?" I challenged.

"He did the deed. What are words compared with that? And even while he was doing it, he cautioned poor Betsy never to speak to any one of it. If she did and she was believed, he would be forced to leave the farm. To leave Tennessee. Her mother would die of shame. Richard and Joel would be orphans. The family would be destroyed because of her selfishness. 'You are the flesh of my flesh, the blood of my blood,' Old Jack told her. 'I am your father, and I can do with you what I please.'"

I exclaimed my outrage. The demon merely laughed.

"And how long was it before you came to save Betsy?" I asked.

"The fourth time."

"John Bell knew his daughter four times?"

"No. Twice. On his third visit, he was frightened away by a noise of rocks being thrown against the house."

"Your doing."

"No. We think by Old Kate Batts's little nigger boys, just as Jack suspected at first. But, whoever it was, they scared Old Jack something fierce. He hied it out of poor Betsy's room with his cod waving high in the air."

"And the fourth time?"

"That time we made the noise. The fourth, fifth, and sixth times. And then Old Jack gave up and never came back. But it was too late for poor Betsy. And that made it too late for Old Jack."

The room then reverberated with a revival of all the noises the spirit had ever made. Betsy, meantime, sat as quietly as she had when I began questioning her. As in the days of her youth, her lips did not move.

181

While I listened to the raucous display, I began to know that I had indeed unlocked the key to the "Bell witch" haunting. Betsy was, in the truest sense, its mother. It was born of the sinful union between father and daughter, but not of flesh. It came from the daughter's desperate need for protection. Several of us in the community had correctly posited that the demon had gone through a birth and adolescent period before it could talk. As with a real child once it is born, this supernatural creation was of the mother but not the mother. It could roam the world as a free and independent spirit, and yet its permanent home was inside Elizabeth Bell Powell. Most amazingly, even though she had been placed in Dr. Mesmer's waking sleep, she was still disconnected from the thing, or at least disconnected to the extent that she could not answer questions on its behalf. Nor, I believe, could she command it to come out and speak. This it had done by itself. Your dear mother and my beloved wife contained at once a trinity: who she was awake, who she was in an unconscious state, and that spirit born of her mind which had become the "Bell witch."

One epiphany after another came upon me in a nerve-wracking rush:

Lucy Bell admitted to being a very sound sleeper, thus giving her husband ample opportunity to sneak off to his daughter's room.

The being was as high-spirited and playful as its mother, as witty and clear of memory as had been my best pupil. It could not answer my questions in Latin or Greek because Betsy knew nothing of these languages. But it had also possessed many nasty and evil attributes, no doubt born of the evil of incest. These qualities had

182

kept me from seeing the gifts Betsy had contributed to its creation.

At the trial brought on by Kate Batts, I know that John was more determined to be found innocent to preserve his community standing than to keep from paying Kate back money. The appearance of being a paragon among his community obsessed him. He was being crushed by the impending trial and the spectre of church excommunication when he first went to Betsy's bedroom. Perhaps it was the threat of a double public disgracing that convinced him he did not in fact possess the goodness to resist so base a passion. I do not know. Perhaps, as he said to me on the day when he privately worried that the spirit could read minds, it is known only to God.

The stage had been set in Red River for a supernatural visitation by a series of strange events. First, a large black animal chanced into the area. Then a large, unknown type of bird. Finally, some girl in a green dress was seen by Betsy swinging from a tree, and she vanished. She might simply have been from a pioneer family passing through the area, pausing to water their horses in the Red River. All of these I believe were natural and explicable and would not have made that great an impression on Betsy, had the family not owned Negroes who thrived on empowering the supernatural world. And had Elizabeth Bell not been at that very time coming into womanhood. As Dr. Mize pointed out during his visit to the Bell farm, there have been many examples of noisy, ghostlike hauntings throughout the history of the world, and most of these have been closely associated with a girl changing into a woman. Some day, science may discover a tremendous unleashing of spiritual force accompanying the first flow of menstrual blood. This is certainly beyond my ken, but I do know that it occurs and definitely did so with your mother.

As to why the entity called itself Kate Batts's witch there is no doubt in my mind. I personally witnessed the effect that old harridan had on young Betsy when she invoked her curse upon John Bell during the camp meeting in Fort's meeting house. Unwittingly, the real Kate sealed her fate in the community when she declared that more than John among the Bells would suffer from her curse. Betsy was attacked by the spirit, I believe, because of this pronouncement and also because her still childish mind believed to a degree her father's words that she held partial blame for his carnal attacks upon her.

It was perhaps not that night but certainly not long afterward that I realized the "witch" had several times told us a great truth about its mother: "I am the spirit of someone who was once happy and who has been disturbed." Hearing the word "spirit," we all naturally were thinking of the ghost of someone dead . . . an explorer or an Indian. But it was Elizabeth Bell who had been happy, until her father visited her on those dark winter nights. Only after those visits had the spirit been born.

People correctly observed that the "witch" was most often around Betsy and generally followed her when she fled to the homes of others. Elizabeth Bell was and remains the spirit's home. They were not correct, however, that she was maliciously creating the "witch." Once it was born, it had total independence from her, to the extent that it could not only fly from her to a great distance but also fly to two places at the same time. Also, one can plainly understand how the creature's attacks on Betsy were in one sense desired, as it gave her an excuse to always keep her mother, sister, or girl friend beside her, as guarantee that her father could never again pay her a midnight visit.

I recalled in a revelatory flash also the dislike of Negroes that both Betsy and the spirit shared. How or why this one mean-spirited aspect of your mother developed, I am at a loss to say. Given all her good features, I have never had the temerity to openly take her to task over this.

Once I had unlocked your mother's mind through Mesmerism, I asked myself again and again how all of us in Red River could have missed the multitude of patent clews. How much clearer could have been the fact that, as Betsy's fits became stronger and stronger, so did the swelling of John's tongue and the twitching of his facial muscles? Or that, once her father was afflicted with his physical torments on a daily basis, that Betsy's fits gradually died away? What would be a natural consequence of a man torn between hiding his most heinous crime and, at the same time, bound by all his religious beliefs to confess and lay his burden upon the Lord? What else but a tongue that swelled so much he could not speak even if he wished to? A tongue that simultaneously concealed his sin and punished him to the point of death by preventing him from taking sustenance? Was this not what John Bell meant by sins known only to God when he visited me that early morning in the school house? Did Dr. Hopson not tell us again and again that John had no physical causes for his sufferings, that the swellings and twitchings were from an illness of his mind? When John let the community know he was suffering physical pains almost daily, why had I not cast my thoughts back to his first attack of swollen tongue, when he was with me at Lawyer

Byrns's house? Knowing what I did, why had I not connected this with my having let John know Betsy had told me about the noises in her bedroom? I truly believe that we of Red River were not all of such simple minds that none could guess the truth. Rather, we wanted to believe that John Bell was the same noble person he wanted so desperately to be. Our hearts would not allow us to know what our eyes saw and our ears heard.

Why would the spirit feel such compassion and solicitude towards Lucy Bell when the woman made no show whatsoever of like feelings towards the spirit? Was this not because of its sympathy for the cheated wife? For all I know, Lucy Bell may have been one who guessed at the cause of the spirit's origin and its persecution of John Bell. Perhaps, as with myself and others of Red River, she could not bring herself to face what she knew in her heart to be the truth of it. Or perhaps, being a woman with small children in a hostile land, she had no choice but to accept what had happened and to let the fantastic retribution play out as it was ordained.

Much will always remain a mystery, because the spirit would only answer so much. This is the balance of our bizarre dialogue:

"Was it nightshade in the bottle?" I asked, after it had pronounced that the rapes had sealed John's doom.

"Yes, yes, yes!"

"And how did the liquid get inside John?"

"We made Betsy pick the berries. She found the bottle empty in the mud beside the Red River. We made her press the berries very carefully, so as not to stain her hands. We made her pour the liquid into the bottle. And we made her pour the liquid down her father's lips while

186

he slept. But she also was in a sleep while all this happened. She remembers none of it. She is innocent."

"If she is innocent and poor Betsy, then why did you pull her hair, slap her face, and embarrass her?"

"She should have spoken out. She should have told her mother and the ministers."

"But, as John said, that would have destroyed her family," I argued.

"Truth carries its price. She held back the truth, and so she was punished."

"And what about Joshua Gardner?"

"What about Joshua Gardner?" it said, using my voice and making the words sound like an echo.

"Why did you forbid Betsy to marry him?"

"Because she would always have been unhappy. I did not forbid her until I was sure it was you she truly loved. She was attracted to you since the day you moved into Red River. But, like you, she feared the great differences in your ages. And then, once Jack got through with her, she feared the physical attentions of an older man. But I kept every one else away from her until the difference of age was not so great. And until you could prove to her that you are a gentle man. I said many times that I loved Betsy, and this is my proof."

"And that is why you tried to force me to come between them and help break the engagement?"

"Even with a push you remained the timid mouse. When you rode up to the pick-nick on the Red River, when Betsy wore Josh's ring, I expected you at last to become eloquent on your own behalf."

"I was," I exclaimed. "Well, perhaps not as eloquent as I should have been, but at least I did plead my case and with great fervour. Betsy could not embarrass Josh, and I was compelled to cease my arguments."

"So that I was compelled shortly thereafter to plead my own case and save her for you."

It laughed again. Betsy's placid face never changed expression, as if she were sitting in an otherwise empty room of a house on the other side of the state.

"Do you expect me to thank you for your kindness?"

"And why not?"

"Because you made my wife a murderess. Why did you not simply speak out on her behalf if she refused to? Why did you not let the court condemn John Bell, as it had in the affair with Kate Batts?"

"No. Old Jack committed his sins in silence. He had ample chance to confess after I appeared, but he did not. Confession was his job, or Betsy's. Mine was retribution, and I took it with leisure. I used that dim-witted Frank Miles to prove to Old Jack that he couldn't fly from me, so that he was obliged to stay at the site of his crime until he died. I let him keep up the sham of his piety, so that he could go through the lip service of his faith at the home altar every day. I let him go on deceiving all the friends who staunchly defended him. I let him taste Hell on earth, to torment him in life before I finally let him go to the Hell of death. You think I am a monster?"

"I cannot judge you," I answered. "You are not of the flesh and beyond my ability to grasp."

"That is wise. Do not waste your time in judging me," it counseled. "I wish to say nothing else to you. Ask me one more question, and then let me go."

"And if I do not care to let you go?" I dared.

Suddenly, my body felt as if a hundred pins were being

stuck in me. I jumped up from the chair with every muscle burning. The spirit laughed in a multitude of its voices.

"One last question," it offered again.

"Very well. How can I convince Betsy that my daughter is safe?"

"Whilst she sleeps you cannot. Stay in your bedroom, close by her side. Do not go out to the necessary in the night. Use the chamber pot. Give her no cause to summon us from her sleep. We wish peace as much as you do. Our work is done. Now let us go."

"But what if my daughter is courted by a young man not of Betsy's liking?" I asked. "Would she not summon you then?"

"Let us go," the voice said, as if from the far end of a hall. It had a pleading tone, as described to me when it begged Betsy not to marry Josh Gardner.

"Very well. Go. Sleep in peace and never return," I said.

The room became very silent. I did what the French nobles had instructed to rouse your mother from Mesmer's sleep. As is most often the case with subjects, she remembered nothing. I did as the spirit advised and did not leave the bedroom at night. It has never reappeared.

Of course, your mother still knows nothing of this remarkable evening. I have kept it and its dark secrets locked inside me all these years. But I fear this private possession, indeed the very act of obtaining what I have here set down, has exacted a dread price. Just as Odin paid for the gift of knowledge at the cost of one eye,[23] the shock of what I learned I am convinced brought on my stroke only a few nights later.

I wonder how much a man might learn if he lived a

thousand years. It has always seemed such a shame that each of us labours a lifetime to build up a priceless store of knowledge, only to have it disappear from the world at the moment of death. I assume the point of this painful, lifelong process of learning will become clear on the other side of the portal. At least one may find comfort in the fact that so many of the wisest thoughts and most profound discoveries have been captured in letters and books.

What prompted the above thoughts was that, despite my enfeeblement from the stroke, the gift of continued life allowed me to gain two other important perspectives on the "Bell witch" troubles. One was from Mr. Webb, whom you know and who visited me about a year after my confinement. He it was who brought a new verse to the Epworth ghost tale first heard from Dr. Mize. Remember that a common characteristic to all Mize's tales was that the case became so celebrated that persons with analytical minds and reputations beyond reproach were always brought in to investigate. We had not heard this in the one case of the Epworth ghost, and yet once again it was true. The personage in this instance was Mr. Joseph Priestley, the scientist who discovered oxygen. Upon studying this case in the most minute detail, Priestley opined the following: Even though Hetty, one of the daughters of Samuel Wesley, may have been the creator of the incident, she had done this unconsciously. In her waking mind she would never have wished such an embarrassing and painful affair upon her family, but in her sleeping mind she was jealous of her brothers' fame and secretly wanted as much attention. And so her unconscious, needful mind created and set loose the invisible beast to wreak vengeance. Would that Dr. Mize had known this key element of the Epworth haunting!

The second insight I gleaned while reading a journal article on the musical genius Wolfgang Amadeus Mozart. According to this scholarly piece, when Mozart was still a lad and touring Europe with his father to make money off his precocious skills, he chanced to visit Rome. Because of his fame he was allowed the rare treat of listening to the sacred Mass setting that was sung only in the Sistine Chapel and only when the pope himself celebrated the Mass. This musical offering was more than a hundred years old. Once its voice parts had been learned in their entirety the music had been destroyed, that no other chapel or church in the world might duplicate it. Replacement singers were taught their part only, through a laborious process of listening over and over until they had it perfectly. The music of this Mass lasted a total of about twenty minutes and was quite complex. Nevertheless, after only that one hearing the young Mozart went back to his hotel and wrote out all voices of the Mass onto score paper, just as an exercise!

If a male mind once every hundred years or so is capable of such a feat, why should the mind not just as rarely in some specially gifted (or cursed) young woman be capable of creating an alternate, invisible wish being?

To me this is not a rhetorical question; I personally have witnessed that it happens.

Even before I suffered my stroke, I was well aware of the fragility of life, that one may be here one minute and for ever gone the next. Thus I have laboured long to set all this down, first in haste and then later in detail, driven by the fear that I will be gone and your mother will remarry, bringing another man under this roof. Or that my unanswered question will come to pass when you will inevitably welcome suitors, any one of whom may be regarded in your mother's sleeping mind as a threat to you. Then the spirit would rise again, and it might give the two of you no wisdom to deal with its wrath. This was the impetus for all my writing.

I thank God that He did not enfeeble my pen hand and that He gave me the many months necessary to set all of this down. While our riches have dwindled, He has also been kind enough to grant me the extra years to see you blossom into womanhood. You are wise beyond your years. Armed with the knowledge in this recounting, I am confident that you and your mother will be safe from the "Bell witch" when I am gone. If you have chosen to read this out of curiosity and the spirit has not returned, do not share it with any one. This would surely kill your mother, long before the possibility that she might be judged by the law to account for the murder of her father. Once your mother is reunited with me in Heaven, the choice of what to do with this is yours. Perhaps you, like the rest of the Bell family, will not want to shoulder the burdens of this fearsome tale. I hope, however, that you will have the courage to see that it is made public. There is much that can and should be learned here.

Your loving father

Notes

━━━━━━━━━

1. Ralph Winters, *Historical Sketches/Adams/Robertson County/and/Port Royal/Montgomery County Tennessee/1779–1968* (Clarkesville, Tenn.: Samuel Winters, 1978). Winters writes that Fort's meeting house was a frame building 40 x 28 feet, begun on Feb. 15, 1817. He cites church records: on May 17, 1817, "The Commissioners reported the building ready [so] the church agreed that the Commissioners go on and have a low division made in the S. E. corner which is alloted [sic] to the Negroes. Also to have the house filled with new benches and a new pulpit. One door with lock and key—the other bolted inside" (p. 88).

2. According to *Webster's New World Dictionary*, an anxious seat is "a bench near the preacher at revival meetings, for those with a troubled conscience who seek salvation." Herman A. Norton, in his chapter on Revivalism in *Religion in Tennessee/1777–1945* (Knoxville: The Tennessee Historical Commission/The University of Tennessee Press, 1981), writes:

    The tremendous excitement that characterized the revival in Tennessee was accompanied by strange manifestations never before witnessed in the area. . . . The "falling exercise" was the most common of all forms of bodily excitement. Amid sobs, moans, cries, some worshipers would be struck down with violent motions of the body. Those who fell would sometimes lie for hours helpless and apparently unconscious of what was going on around them. . . . The "jerking exercise" was also quite common and was the one that spread most rapidly through a congregation. Even preachers were not immune. The jerking exercise affected different persons in different ways. Frequently only one of the limbs would be involved, sometimes the whole body, and often only the head alone. Occasionally those who were seized would be thrown violently to the ground, yet they reported the experience to be one of the happiest of their lives. . . . Related to falling and jerking were rolling, running, dancing, and barking exercises. The barking exercise, where persons went down on all fours and barked until they grew hoarse, made a lasting impression. It was not uncommon to see people gathered around a tree, barking, yelping, "treeing the devil" (pp. 23–25).

3. Winters, op. cit, p. 68. Under "Schools of the Adams Area," "The records of early schools are very scarce. Between 1810 and 1820 there was a Prof. Powell in the area[.] Also in this approximate era Geraldus Pickering is reported to have taught a school here."

4. Gentry R. McGee, Superintendent of City Schools, Jackson, Tennessee, wrote a civics book entitled *A History of Tennessee/From 1663 to 1930* (facsimile reproduction; Nashville: Charles Elder, 1971). In it, he devotes Chapter 11 to the State of Franklin (pp. 78–83). In August 1784, a general convention met at Jonesboro, formed a constitution, and started a new government. ". . . and the new state was named Franklin. Frankland was first proposed, but it was changed to Franklin in honor of Dr. Benjamin Franklin." Internal political rivalries and the failure of North Carolina

and the United States Congress to recognize the state resulted in its expiration in March 1788.

5. Powell's frequent noting of exact dates bears out his claim that he kept a careful log of the haunting. Days of the week which he links to dates prove invariably correct.

6. As mentioned in the introduction, the "Bell witch" cave can still be explored. Sometime in the early twentieth century, what looked to me to be about an acre of land collapsed some twenty feet into what must have been an enormous chamber, due west of where the Bell homestead stood. This place would surely be a pond, were there not numerous passages through the limestone directly down to the Red River.

7. So many incidents of Richard Powell's account parallel those of Charles Bailey Bell and Richard Williams Bell that pages could be spent in cross-reference. Powell's mention of "Old Sugar Mouth" (compare *The Bell Witch/or/Our Family Trouble* (Nashville, Mini-Histories: 1985, pp. l4–l5) is one in which details are especially corroborated by the later accounts.

8. Gentry McGee (op. cit.) writes of Indian fighting: "So many and so fierce had been the battles in this region that the part of it which lies between the Cumberland and the Ohio rivers was called "The Dark and Bloody Ground," or, in the Indian tongue, "Kentucky."

9. Ronald N. Satz, *Tennessee's Indian Peoples/From White Contact to Removal, 1540–1840,* (Knoxville: The Tennessee Historical Commission/The University of Tennessee Press, 1979):

> The Woodland people [ca. 1,000 B.C.] were the first Indians of Tennessee to build mounds, many of which may still be seen in the state—some of them created by Woodland Indians, others by their descendants of later tradition. Those built by Woodland Indians are burial mounds: dome-shaped earthen tombs for the dead. But not all people of the Woodland tradition were buried in mounds.

Scholars are not certain of why some individuals were given these elaborate burials and others were not, but it is obvious that a complex social and religious structure was in operation, affecting to some degree the lives of most Woodland Indians. (p. 6)

10. Norton's *Religion in Tennessee* confirms Powell's observations.
11. Corn rock: an early attempt at automation. After a field was plowed, the farmer walked the rows poking holes every foot or so with a long dibble. If he had a wife, or a child old enough to walk, they followed behind him, dropping a kernel of corn into each hole. The farmer would then close the holes by hitching a large, flat rock to his horse and dragging it up and down the rows.
12. It is purely coincidental that John Bell's condition bears some resemblance to Bell's palsy. The latter condition was described by Scottish anatomist Sir Charles Bell, who specialized in investigations of the human brain and nervous system. The term did not come into popular usage until the l860s, long after John Bell's death. According to the *Encyclopaedia Britannica,* 1971, vol. 17, p. 315:

> Bell's palsy is a peripheral neuritis of unknown cause affecting a single nerve trunk—the facial nerve—and resulting in paralysis of all the muscles of one side of the face. It is usually rapid in onset; on the affected side the facial lines are smoothed out, the forehead cannot be wrinkled or the eye closed, and the corner of the mouth droops. . . . In the majority of cases recovery occurs, though it may take many months.

13. Evidently, this event was kept very well "hushed," as it does not appear in any later account.
14. "One of the earliest doctors of the area was possibly Dr. Hopson. We have a record where he attended John Bell in his last illness in 1819. Bell lived about 7 miles up the river near where the present Adams is located." Winters, op. cit., p. 27.

15. Lester C. Lamon's *Blacks in Tennessee/1791–1970* (Knoxville, The Tennessee Historical Commission/The University of Tennessee Press, 1981) provides a wealth of information to back up and illuminate Dick Powell's tale. Among these: "The white population [in Tennessee] grew by 137 percent between 1800 and 1810, and the slave population by a dramatic 238 percent"; blacks "lived and worked closely with whites, and the regularity of personal contact tended to downplay the importance of enforcing racially restrictive legislation"; "Slaves on the early Tennessee frontier rarely lived in groups, for most slaveholders owned only one or two slaves, or perhaps a slave family. Farms were isolated, and slave and master shared many common experiences. Together, they herded cattle and hogs, cleared land, built barns, attended church, and kept an alert eye for hostile Indians"; "Slaves in these early days were rarely sold." In 1820, the census showed that Middle Tennessee had 67,445 black slaves, 1,559 free blacks, and 221,670 whites (pp. 6–10 and Appendix).

16. Ralph Winters, op. cit., p. 12, writes: "The earliest forms of transportation from Port Royal were flat boats which carried various farm products and produce to Natchez, Mississippi, and New Orleans, Louisiana. These log rafts would be built during summer and fall and loaded in winter ready for a "high rise" to carry them down stream. Usually two men went on each raft and when the cargo was sold they would then sell the logs or raft and walk or buy a horse and ride through the wilderness back home. Travelling the Natchez Trail many of them were robbed and/or killed."

17. *Webster's New World Dictionary* gives one definition of "sawyer" as "a log or tree caught in a river so that its branches saw back and forth with the water." Evidently, Samuel Clemens borrowed more than his own pen name, Mark Twain, from Mississippi river jargon.

18. Bell, book, and candle. Some time between the middle of the eighth century and the end of the ninth century arose a formal rite of excommunication in the Roman Catholic Church. This

involved ringing the church bells, reading from and then closing the Bible, and having twelve priests dash their candles to the ground, extinguishing them. Centuries later, a corrupted form of the rite was used against witches.

19. Apollo is probably not the man's first name. Andrew Jackson was an educated man and, as such, must have been aware of Greek mythology. Apollo was the god of death from afar, terror, and awe.

20. Additional proof that John Bell's affliction was not Bell's palsy, as his "face fairly danced hour after hour with contortions." Further, although it did not yet have the name of the Scottish anatomist, the condition of Bell's palsy might well have been known by someone in the community.

21. In the first half of the nineteenth century, the diamond was rarely used in engagement rings; emeralds were more common.

22. From *Benjamin Franklin* by Ronald W. Clark (New York: Random House, 1983):

> Five doctors were ordered to investigate Mesmer's claim, and Franklin was shortly afterward asked for his own views by M. de la Condamine. "I think that, in general, maladies caused by obstructions may be treated by electrcity with advantage," he replied. "As to the animal magnetism so much talked of, I must doubt its existence till I can see or feel some effect of it. None of the cures said to have been performed by it have fallen under my observation, and there being so many disorders which cure themselves and one another on these occasions, and living long has given me so frequent opportunity of seeing certain remedies cried up as curing everything, and yet soon after totally laid aside as useless, I cannot but fear that the expectation of great advantage from this new method of treating diseases will prove a delusion. That delusion may, however, and in some cases, be of use while it lasts. There are in every great, rich city a number of persons who are never in health, because they are fond of medicines and always

taking them, whereby they derange the natural functions and hurt their constitution. If these people can be persuaded to forbear their drugs, in expectation of being cured by only the physician's finger, or an iron rod pointing at them, they may possibly find good effects, though they mistake the cause'' (p. 39).

23. Powell was just as capable of calling up mythological metaphors as was General Jackson. According to Edith Hamilton, in her *Mythology/Timeless Tales of Gods and Heroes* (New York: New American Library, 1940): Odin ''was the All-father, supreme among the gods and men, yet even so he constantly sought for more wisdom. He went down to the Well of Wisdom, guarded by Mimir the wise, to beg for a draught from it, and when Mimir answered that he must pay for it with one of his eyes, he consented to lose the eye'' (p. 308).